D1519958

The Field of Play

A Guide
for the Theory and Practice
of Music Therapy

Carolyn Bereznak Kenny

The Field of Play

*A Guide
for the Theory and Practice
of Music Therapy*

Carolyn Bereznak Kenny

Ridgeview Publishing Company

Paper text: ISBN 0-917930-50-9
Cloth (Library edition): ISBN 0-917930-97-5

The illustrator, who did the cover, the full color
plate, and all the numbered diagrams, is M. Carmen
Marcus.

Published in the United States of America
by Ridgeview Publishing Company
Box 686
Atascadero, California   93423

Printed in the United States of America
by Ridgeview Letterpress & Offset, Inc.
Independence, Ohio   44131

Contents

vi

Acknowledgements

Acknowledgements to copyright holders for permission to reprint passages go to:

Helen L. Bonny for permission to reprint a figure from "The Role of Taped Music Programs in the GIM Process" (ICM Books, Baltimore, MD: 1978).

Helen L. Bonny and Pergamon Press, Inc for permission to reprint a passage from "Music: The Language of Immediacy," in *The Arts in Pyschotherapy*, vol. 14, 1987.

Barbara Hesser for permission to reprint passages from the *Proceedings from the International Symposium on Music in the Life of Man: Toward a Theory of Music Therapy* (New York University: 1982).

E.P. Dutton for permission to reprint a passage
from George Leonard, *The Silent Pulse* (E. P. Dutton, New York: 1978).

Pantheon Books for permission to reprint a passage from Jonathan Miller, *States of Mind* (Pantheon Books, New York: 1983).

Charles T. Eagle for permission to reprint a figure from *The Music Psychology Index*, vol. 2, 1978.

MMB Music for permission to reprint passages from Even Ruud, *Music Therapy and Its Relationship to Current Treatment Theories* (MMB Music, St. Louis: 1980).

Shambhala Publications for permission to reprint a passage from Jose Arguelles, *Earth Ascending: An Illustrated Treatise on the Law Governing Whole Systems* 1984) and for permission to reprint a passage from *The Holographic Paradigm and Other Paradoxes* edited by Ken Wilber (1982). Reprinted by arrangement with Shambhala Publications, Inc., 300 Massachusetts Ave., Boston, MA 02115.

Bernard Feder for permission to reprint passages
from Feder E. and Feder B., *The Expressive Arts Therapies* (Prentice Hall, Englewood Cliffs, NJ: 1981).

Macmillan Publishing Company for permission to reprint passages from E. Thayer Gaston, *Music in Therapy* (Macmillan Publishing Company,

Dedication

I dedicate this book to my children Shannon and Josh and to my parents Sam and Ruth, who through their inspiration and their love have offered me the two most essential ingredients for my work and for my life.

I also dedicate this book to the Phoenicians.

In ancient times there was a great mythical bird, called the Phoenix, who rose gloriously out of the ashes of destruction and served as a magnificent and powerful symbol of our ability to create new life out of death.

In the history of mankind the Phoenicians were a brave and adventurous people who explored the vast territory of the unknown seas.

In my life the Phoenicians are a small and dedicated community of visionaries and dreamers who gather for five days every summer and retreat into the arms of the Mother herself in the New York Catskill Mountains to meditate, explore the power of sound, share dreams and visions of a better world for the human person and of our role in the creative process of human development.

Of these Phoenicians, I would especially like to

acknowledge Barbara Hesser, Helen Bonny, Even Ruud, David Burrows, Lisa Summer, Sara Jane Stokes, Joanne Crandall, David Gonzales, Lisa Sokolov, Clive and Carol Robbins, Liz Moffitt, Rachael Verney, John Marcus.

In addition, I extend my gratitude to the University of Quebec in Montreal for creating the time and space for the writing of this book and, in particular, to my friend and colleague, Connie Isenberg-Grezda. I would also like to thank the many colleagues, students, clients and friends, who each in their own way have participated in the creation of *The Field of Play*.

For personal support and encouragement, thanks go to Rich Appelbaum, Judith Lazerson, Cliff Leonard, and Helen Vreeland.

Foreward

It is an old theoretical tradition within the field of music therapy to consider music as part of a broader system of health. Until the last century when the term 'health' meant more than physical well-being music was thought of as an important way of regulating man's relation to the world.

Carolyn Kenny revisits this lost tradition in her new book. Some music therapists may say that music therapy has outgrown this ancient speculative tradition. Those trained in a school of thought valuing prediction and measurement may not appreciate that there are contemporary music therapists insisting on keeping these broader cultural traditions alive. These music therapists are concerned that the creation of a primarily technological field could contribute to the removal of music from our everyday life experience and overall quality of life, thus leaving the cultural industry the task of providing music as another commodity in a consumers' market.

One might ask the question: If you have seen that music therapy works, why set out to prove it? Isn't this rather the time to develop *our understanding* of how musical involvement helps to structure the

xiv

experience of the person seeking change?

To work in the tradition of understanding means to learn to perceive. And to learn to perceive is not the same as to learn to observe and measure. Beyond the naive assumptions of positivist theory that what you perceive are "facts," we need to develop our understanding that perceiving always implies theory and that the way we are ordering our realities depends on our categories of thought, our values and our feelings.

Carolyn is one of the few contemporary music therapists who has the courage to develop this understanding and its implications for our field. Carolyn, as I have learned to know her, is also one of those few theorists in our field who includes more than one modality in her categories of thought.

If you listen to this book you may learn that it is possible to conceive of music therapy processes in that rich complexity which music unfolds, those sometimes paradoxical processes needing multi-dimensional representation. You may also learn that understanding the nature of music, the *Field of Play*, means creating a new language upon which to grasp more fully the processes leading towards human change.

Even Ruud, Ph.D.

Preface

In our day we have the good fortune to observe and participate in one of the most exciting and brilliant transformations in the history of mankind. We are blossoming into a world where art and science are coming to a table where there is a great feast.

The feast consists of the many processes and products which will emerge out of a paradoxical dialogue between two worlds, which on the surface appear to be a different as the sun and the moon, day and night.

By nature, the music therapist is required daily to walk between these two worlds, much as the ancient shaman, who was required to dance the great dance between spirit and matter.

In the morning light there is a delicate and gentle sense of beginnings, a promise, a song. It is in these first moments of time that we can touch and taste and hear the horizon of our tomorrows.

The music therapist is one of the keepers of the gate, one of the technicians of the sacred, one who sees the vision and hears the song of the one and the many, the one who dances on the edge of time, one who can guard the threshold of being, one who waits for sound...

Carolyn B. Kenny

Chapter one

Introduction

The Burning Question
The State of the Art
Language and Description

It is in those moments of silence, just as
they begin to unfold into sound again—at
the other side of the human vocabulary—It
is those moments of silence, after the
perfect blending of sound in music—when
all things are not only possible, but are
coexistent. When you break the barriers of
limitation, necessary limitations—through the
barriers of limitations into All—That—Is. It
is then that *Music becomes the language of
immediacy...*
(From Helen L. Bonny "Reflections: Music,
the Language of Immediacy")

The Burning Question

I suppose there are a handful of significant moments in careers of music therepists when research questions are born. Sometimes these questions have a very short life—something like five minutes or a day.

Being inclined toward reflection and having an on-going questioning attitude, I have experienced many of these questions springing out of the work.

Some questions have consumed and generated more energy than others. A few have had a long life. Some have been posed from outside sources.

Questions press the accountability button.

For example, in order for the Canadian government to fund a demonstration project demonstrating "the effectiveness of music therapy", in institutions in Vancouver, British Columbia in the mid-seventies, it was necessary for our music therapy practice to expand itself into a full-fledged research project. Our team included two fulltime music therapists, one fulltime research psychologist, one half-time research psychologist/social worker and another consulting research psychologist.

Our burning question was: Is music therapy effective?

This research question generated a 225-page document entitled *The Music Therapy Evaluation Study*, filled to the brim with results of standardized tests, questionnaires, check lists quotes from patient diaries and rating scales. In addition, there were approximately 50 hours of videotapes and one 16 mm documentary film entitled "Listen to the Musicmakers."

The question got answers not only on paper and film, but certainly in the lives of many clients served through funding by Health and Welfare Ottawa. It also yielded results in helping to establish music therapy training and practice not only in Vancouver, British Columbia, but across Canada as well.

Then there are other questions, which remain on-going, or even more often, merely generate more questions. These are the more difficult ones because they seem illusive, almost invisible and yet deeper. Just when you think you've got it, something moves and everything changes. These are the questions which most challenge our creativity, our faith in the work.

I have had a few of these questions as well.

For example: Why do patients in two psychiatric clinics in the Health Sciences Centre Hospital at the University of British Columbia in Vancouver, British Columbia, in the majority, consistently over a two-year period, express and communicate themes of death and rebirth regardless of which music therapy technique is employed?

This particular question catapulted me into the mythic dimension—a study of transformation, ancient healing rituals, the enduring developmental patterns of human nature over time and a Master's thesis entitled "The Death Rebirth Myth as the Healing Agent in Music." This work, in turn, led to *The Mythic Artery: The Magic of Music Therapy.*

Seven years later I met Debbie, and yet another

research question was born.

Debbie was an accident victim with severe physical disabilities and serious brain damage. She had been sent to our convalescent hospital from a rehabilitation center because of her lack of response to rehabilitation treatment. She had not spoken for 2 years. I worked with her in music therapy, doing musical improvisation at the piano, 2 to 3 times a week, for half hour sessions over one and a half years. After a few months she began "sounding" with her voice. At the end of the first year, she began to speak. Her first word was "piano." Then she progressed to singing, and so the story goes. I was deeply moved by this experience.

There were four elements which contributed to the new question. First, I needed to find a way to share the process of that experience without distorting or taking away from it—without losing the immediacy and vibrant movement of that dance we sounded in the music, in the relationships. A verbal language was not available in my field of music therapy, or in others.

Second, in June of 1982 I participated in one of a series of International study groups, this one a symposium at New York University entitled "Music in the Life of Man: Toward a Theory of Music Therapy." Our task was "to develop principles on what is inherent in the experience of music which makes it unique in therapy."

Thirty-six music therapists and music psychologists gathered from 20 countries to engage in a think tank about the state of the art in music therapy. We each had written a position paper, which had been circulated to the symposium members prior to the gathering. I had written about Debbie.

One point of agreement, after our 6-day intensive, was the shared frustration of lack of language in which to discuss the music therapy experience. The statement from the Research/Client Assessment group was:

> In summary, there were no conclusions drawn as to effective methods for analyzing and presenting publicly the use of clinical piano improvisation. There was a sense of frustration that this material was not being shared effectively. This seemed to stem from the difficulty of objectively describing what happened within the session. (*Proceedings from the International Symposium on Music in the Life of Man*, 1982)

This problem was essentially due to the non-verbal nature of the art. Yet we remained firmly committed to the idea that there were essential elements inherently contained in the music therapy experience. If we began the task of theory-building, however slowly, the result would reap rewards not only for music therapy but also for psychology and human development.

This was the fuel I needed to motivate me in my present research: a shared group commitment, a supportive network, a common information and experience base, a sense of mystery and a global endeavor.

The third element is the continuation of previous questions. I had satisfied my curiosity about "effects." I had no outside funding sources demanding replication. Now I could focus on inner questions—the difficult ones, the ones concerning "process." This meant dealing with problems of language for description of systems, designing of soft theoretical frameworks, recovering ancient concepts with an eye for future vision.

The fourth element is my desire to create ritual structures for the enactment of healing myths, musical myths. In *Myths to Live By*, Joseph Campbell put forth a rationale for the creation of new myths for out time. I was challenged by this possibility.

My first book, *The Mythic Artery: The Magic of Music Therapy* was the first stage in this process for me. I had identified music as carrying implicit *healing patterns* for human development, identified spontaneously by patients in a psychiatric setting. In this earlier work, I had subsequently focused on the "death-rebirth myth." The "Field of Play" brings the content of myth (an exemplary journey or inspirational story communicating human constants even in pure sound), into an abstract ritual form, for use in healing, with a range of techniques and clientele.

Eliade (1963) said that myths are in the realm of sacred time and space and are exemplary models. Even though the concept of myth is not discussed explicitly in this work, it is implied in that ritual is a vehicle for myth. This theoretical framework is a structure, or in effect, a ritual form, which hopefully can embody the myths of human growth and change and provide a vehicle in which myth can enact itself over time in human experience.

The background for the mythic dimension is contained in *The Mythic Artery: The Magic of Music Therapy*. So, my burning question is: Is it possible to formulate a language to describe the music therapy experience and create one of many possible general models which accurately reflect music therapy process, yet can be understood and used by professionals in other fields?

This question has brought challenge.

After five years of meeting this challenge, the clearest point for me is the idea of the importance of loving and creating. The value of a loving and supportive field which has its goal the creation of beauty seems to me a simple human idea which is clear and unequivocal for any type of development, therapeutic or otherwise.

The importance of sound and image are central to my ideas about healing. Sound moves. Sound forms. Sound changes.

George Leonard, in the *The Silent Pulse*, has said:

> At the root of all power and motion, at the burning center of existence itself, there is music and rhythm, the play of patterned frequencies against a matrix of time. We now know that every particle in the physical universe takes its characteristics from the pitch and pattern and overtones of its particular frequencies, its singing. And the

same is true of all radiation, all forces great
and small, all information. (1978, p. 3)

There is an exquisite beauty in patterns
seemingly unknown, yet sensed, felt and experienced.
These implied patterns are called forth when the
intuitive function has the safety and security of a
supportive field, which encourages the "hearing" and
"recognizing" of these sound patterns. The *creative
process* of human growth and change has a chance to
soar within this field of loving and creating in sound.
My experience in music therapy provides a context in
which to see this creative process in action—and it is
my *unique* perspective, my particular pair of
phenomenological glasses which will view this
experience as a "Field of Play."

By first examining the roots of the theoretical
tradition in the field of music therapy, I hope that my
perspective will emerge partially through an
appreciation of that which has come before me. I
have also searched for "our place" in the philosophy
and theory of science—a perch from which to fly.

Yet hidden beneath the surface of every music
therapy practice of every music therapy practitioner
is a unique theoretical foundation. We may share
some soft structural components, the same
techniques, the same methods. But the psyche or soul
of the work is contained in the individuality of each
and every music therapist. This individuality is a
constant source of nourishment which enables our
work to remain living, moving evolving as a form of
therapy—much like music itself.

State of the Art

Music therapy is a process and a form which combines the healing aspects of music with issues of human need to move toward the health and development of the individual and society-at-large. The music therapist serves as a resource person and guide, providing musical experience which directs clients towards health and well-being (Kenny, 1982).

The field of music therapy began as a clinical practice in the late 1940's with the return of World War II veterans who were unmotivated and depressed. Music emerged as an effective therapeutic tool to improve this condition (Gaston, 1968; Michel, 1976).

Over the next twenty-five years, music therapy became closely aligned with the behavioral sciences. Literature was designed to promote and support the acceptance of clinical practice, which was conducted primarily in state institutions, hospitals for the mentally-ill and facilities for the developmentally disabled (Jellison, 1976; Jorgenson & Parnell, 1970; Madson, 1975; Wolpow, 1976).

Simultaneously a more subtle strain of research was developing which reflected the movement of the culture at large.

There was a questioning of the validity of a reductionist approach, which encouraged the steady link to "observable behavior" (Task Panel Reports, 1978). This movement was spearheaded by studies incorporating the use of psychedelic drugs with music (Bonny, 1975; Bonny & Walter, 1972; Eagle, 1972;

Gaston & Eagle, 1970). Bonny further developed the psychedelic drug studies at the Maryland Psychiatric Institute, emphasizing consciousness (1975; Bonny & Savary, 1973). She implied that there could be something therapeutic or healing in our experience with music which was best described in the realms of consciousness and therefore difficult to observe in concrete and immediate behavior. Bonny designed a model which incorporated her knowledge in music and healing with current humanistic and transpersonal trends searching for the "inner state," which often eludes observation of behavior (See the diagram, on page 11, taken from *The role of taped music programs in the GIM process*). This, too, reflected the dilemma of the psychological sciences in general.

It was time for consciousness to emerge as a major interest of psychology and related fields. Jonathon Miller described this dilemma of the psychological sciences:

> In its understandable effort to be regarded as one of the natural sciences psychology paid the unnecessarily high price of setting aside any consideration of consciousness and purpose in the belief that such concepts would plunge the subject back into a swamp of metaphysical idealism. Research was designed on "positivistic" lines, so that the emphasis inevitably fell on measurable stimuli and observable behavior. It soon became apparent that such a programme could not be sustained and that psychology

ALTERED STATES OF CONSCIOUSNESS

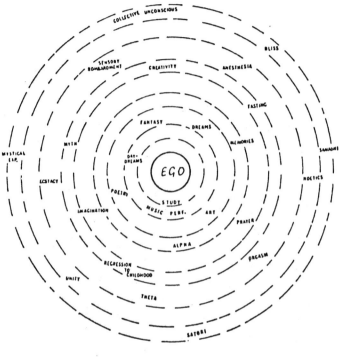

Cut Log Diagram

MEANS:

sleep
meditation
exhaustion
drugs
hypnosis
biofeedback
music
sex
aesthetics

METHODS:

relaxation
concentration

would begin to stagnate if research failed to take account of the inner state of the living being. (1983, p. 32)

The next step was to explore the inner state. According to Jung (1956), the "inner state" finds its entrance into consciousness through art. As early as 1959, Aldous Huxley critiqued our separation from art and advocated a bridge-building between art and science:

> We are on the horns of this dilemma: we need to have the facts of science become tinged with emotion before they can become the material of art, but we need to have them already transformed into the material of art before they can become fully valuable for us in emotional terms. The question is finding a suitable vocabulary in which to deal with these problems. (Huxley, 1973)

His concern was to develop a link between the emotions and a new vocabulary.

The intellectual and professional climate has changed since music therapy had its origins, since Huxley stated his concerns and since Bonny presented her controversial research. This has happened largely because of the inroads created by pioneers in humanistic and transpersonal psychologies, the new physics and the consciousness movement in general (McWhinney, 1984; Ornstein,

1972; Wilber, 1982).

In November, 1985, Bonny presented a paper entitled "Music: The Language of Immediacy" to the National Creative Arts Therapies Association in New York. She stated:

> Information concerning musical stimulation on body systems, neural, muscular, aural are known, at least in relation to medical and biological science. But we are learning that there are other ways in which to probe and investigate the miraculous workings of the human being. The carefully researched and discrete paradigms underlying medical science daily practiced and accepted by our society are not truth per se but *one* of a number of explanations. It occurs to me that the reason we music therapists and other creative therapists cannot find a viable and acceptable modus operendum in attaching our bandwagon to current modalities may be because we are looking in the wrong directions. Like the adventurer who searches the world for treasure and finds it in his own backyard, we may find the diamonds we seek in our own house. (p. 255)

At this point in time, the largest portion of music therapy literature which has accumulated over the last thirty-five years does not really say too much about the inherent processes and experience of music and music therapy. Typical articles reported in

journals read as follows: "A Comparison of Music as Reinforcement for Correct Mathematical Responses Versus Music As Reinforcement for Attentiveness" (Madson, 1975).

This young field does not really have a theory or a methodology.

Some groundwork for theory has been laid. In general these studies indicate an interest in the creation of models which are population-specific (Asmus and Gilbert, 1981; Gfeller, 1984; James, 1984; LeBlanc, 1982; Troup, 1979) and only a few general models. As Bonny has said, we may "seek the diamonds in our own house." We may look closely at music therapy experience and process and speak truly about it from our direct clinical experience, not through the language of other modalities.

According to Charles Eagle, one of the pioneers in music therapy, this is an interdisciplinary field. (See the diagram on page 15.)

Yet there is also something inherent and unique about the experience and process of music which needs to be sought if we are in fact, to allow this experience to help in the formulation of Huxley's "new language" and convey and describe Bonny's "language of immediacy."

There are challenges in naming and describing the music therapy experience. The first is certainly the non-verbal nature of the art. This seems to be the overriding concern of groups such as the *International Symposium on Music in the Life of Man: Toward a Theory of Music Therapy*. The final recommendation of this group of music therapists,

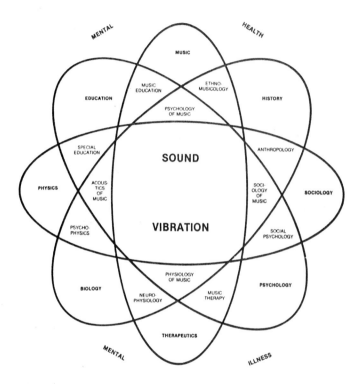

music psychologists, performers and composers was that description be used as a means to determine the foundations of music therapy.

By describing the process, one could discover new aspects of it, and understand it better. The group also acknowledged the element of choice in theory-building:

> The principles of Music Therapy can either be formulated by the support of philosophical and scientific approaches or be determined by our own independent theory of Music Therapy (*Proceedings from the International Symposium on Music in the Life of Man*, 1982)."

They named the components of the musical experience as the following:

1) Social/cultural aspects
2) Neuro-physiological basis
3) Aesthetics
4) Musical Personality of Client/creative process

The group agreed that at least in terms of our field, these studies were in uncharted territory and exploratory in nature. Most participants were committed to designing a musical language in words to describe the musical process. This meant words with movement, words of expansion and an honoring of the process of the musical experience.

The Field of Play emphasizes the importance of

aesthetics, creative process and musical personality of both client and therapist. Although the language of the work is not the language of personality theory, the creative process deals with the development of the whole person, and thus also the development of the personality. The language is the language of music therapy. It does not specifically cover the areas of society and culture or neurophysiology. There are also important links to the fields of physics, biology and the natural sciences, which will not be developed here.

Language and Description

It is important to emphasize the non-verbal nature of the music therapy experience. Trying to describe it or explain it in the "terms" of verbal language, in a sense, must sacrifice some of its essence. And this language and description process seeks "essence."

The best we can expect is to translate our music therapy experience into the language of words, and visual, conceptual images. In this process, we attempt to find appropriate scientific tools to link art and science for the benefit of the clinical community.

A hidden question is: What is the reality of the music therapy experience?

In an article entitled, "Noetic Planning: The Need to Know, But What?", Lionel Livesey Jr. states:

What "reality" ultimately is behind the phenomenon of both subjective and objective

> experience remains beyond the limitations
> and even the interest of science. However,
> it may well be that we have other access to
> this reality in direct experience and its
> sublimation in art, music and mystical
> knowledge. (1972, p. 156)

We also must consider the interdisciplinary nature of
the art.

Even Ruud, the Norwegian theorist and music
therapy educator states:

> The field of Music Therapy can never
> establish theories and procedures separated
> from those within the field of psychology
> and philosophy. It is therefore necessary for
> music therapists to be closely oriented
> towards these disciplines in order to
> maintain this relationship as well as to
> maintain their integrity. The field of Music
> Therapy differs from that of psychology in
> that music therapists are concerned both
> with man and the relationship-man-music.
> In this connection it is to be mentioned
> that this aspect of the field needs special
> care. The relation between man and music
> constitutes the unique part of the discipline
> and gives the field its unique status. (1980,
> p. 70)

In 1980 Ruud described the field of music
therapy as being in Thomas Kuhn's "pre-paradigmatic

phase" and encouraged the designing of models which respected the interdisciplinary nature of the art yet emerged from the unique part of the discipline, the relation between man and music.

> The field of Music Therapy ought to be an open field where different models of understanding are given the possibilities to collaborate with each other. However procedures within the field of therapy with music ought to be judged, not on the basis of whether they are "humanistic," "true," or "scientific," but rather on the basis of their consequences. (Ruud 1980, p. 71)

Ruud proposed that only the testing and application of models will prove their value.

But the deeper and more elusive problem has to do with the element of consciousness. How do sensation and expression relate to feeling, idea, attitude, inspiration, and change? Can music provide an expanding systems model? These questions also emerge from issues of man in relationship to music.

A living system creates an energy flow of expansion, a primary field for growth and change. It is a life-producing model. In *Earth Ascending: An Illustrated Treatise on the Law Governing Whole Systems*, Argüelles addressed the global issue of art and consciousness:

> Art is a function of energy. Given the unity of mankind as a single planetary organism,

art is the expressive connective tissue
binding together the individual organisms
through energy transformations focused in
the emotional centers of those organisms.
Properly catalyzed through form, rhythm,
color, light, sound and movement, emotional
energy is directly related to the establishment of a dynamic equilibrium with the
other forces of the phenomenal world.
(1984, p. 147)

Argüelles took the whole systems perspective.
How do the parts relate to the whole? Yet the Field
of Play takes one step back into considerations of the
field, created by Ruud's "man-relationship-music." It
concentrates on what is unique in the music therapy
experience, and yet may also be reflected in other
experience if we can find a way to translate this
"language of immediacy."

Theory

The problem for any serious artist or educator is to re-create a common language for the communication of...knowledge. We don't have common language because we don't have a common view of the universe we are living in. We don't share premises any more. I don't think we can resurrect any of the traditions in quite their old forms. But we can re-explore these civilizations...retranslate their ideas into forms appropriate to the present. We will re-create our culture by going back to the roots.

(From Kathleen Raines, "Recovering a Common Language")

Why Theory?

Theory serves as a foundation.

Each individual operates from a theoretical base. This base may not be articulated. It may remain unacknowledged, unspoken, unformed, barely in the imagination. Whether articulated or not, we each have an underlying sense of structure at the base of our experience. Whether articulated or not, music therapy, as a field, also has an underlying structure.

In general, theory is abstract. It's goal is to describe the constant elements of our experience. (Every new situation brings new and varied elements into our structures which are specific to the context, yet exude the unseen structure of our theory.)

Theory reflects the "big picture". In Carlos Castaneda's book, *The Power of Silence*, the center piece of the work is a concept called "abstract cores". This means the structure which can hold a million different stories. And of course, there are many choices of "abstract cores."

A theory is something like an abstract core. We learn about it through having many experiences. After a certain number of experiences in a certain field, we begin to notice constants, which pervade our experiences, no matter how varied those experiences may be.

The result of this process of observation, is that the theory, or abstract core, or even schema, can then be recycled back into experience and may assist us in moving on to a new level of understanding and appreciation about our experiences, as we observe ourselves in them.

A theory implies a kind of architecture of thought—a structure of patterns, connections, shapes. In a way, a theory can be imagined to be a symbol of our experience.

We might then interpret our symbol by translating it into words as concepts, principles, elements, constructs.

There are many hazards in the process of theory-building. One of these hazards is particularly significant in the theory-building task for the field of music therapy.

As we examine the roots of theoretical work in music therapy it will bring us home again to another variation in the problematic mind-body split—process versus prodect, linear versus circular, verbal versus non-verbal, logical versus intuitive, explicit versus implicit. This is no surprise since by definition music therapy walks between the two worlds of art and science.

Yet it is time to begin the dialogue between worlds, those two worlds inside each one of us. It is time to begin the exploration into theory, to start the foundation. In most cases, music therapy has looked to outside theory for its support. Perhaps even because of our position "between the worlds", we will have something to offer others, that part which is unique to our experience as music therapists.

The global issue aside, it is important to remember that the primary purpose for a theory is to support the field: music therapy practionners, music therapy educators, music therapy trainees, music therapy researchers, associations, and subsequently those who receive our service.

For years now, whenever I have asked music therapists in all of these categories, what they feel they need to support their work, their reply usually boils down to "a new language" to describe our experience.

The discerning music therapist is cautious in the use of language which describes the work. Perhaps this discernment comes from the non-verbal nature of our discipline, the aesthetic dimension, the importance of intuition, the fact that music itself is another language. Perhaps we are looking for words which express more clearly than usual words, the relationship between the human condition and music, mankind's relationship to sound.

This new language will take a kind of play, a new creation, another aspect of being or dancing or singing between two worlds.

The new language must be so soft and translucent that it can hold a million variations. The process of creation is at the heart of our work and therefore our theories must represent dynamic forms. Solid cannot mean static. Clear cannot mean fixed. And we must "hear" our experience in these theoretical forms, symbols which carry resounding themes.

As we examine the roots of some of the theoretical work in music therapy we ask this question: Can we hear resounding themes of human experience in these words? Can we sense an underlying order? As we each begin the process of exploring our own individual theoretical inclinations, we can ask: Do our words resonate our life with music and people in states of change, healing, humanness, beauty, struggle, resolution, disappointment, joy, love? Is this like our encounter with man and music?

Back to the Roots

Because the roots of music therapy are so firmly established in medicine, a general tendency of theory-building efforts has been to join forces with theories or models which are grounded in the medical field itself and to avoid the discrete context of music therapy. Even Ruud, in his text *Music Therapy and Other Treatment Modalities*, examines the relationship of music therapy to medical models, communication models and general psychological models, many of which also have their origins in medicine.

Ruud describes music therapy as being in Thoman Kuhn's "pre-paradigmatic phase" and encourages the design of models which respect the interdisciplinary nature of the art yet emerge from the unique part of the discipline, the relation between man and music. Ruud directs us to theory formation within the field of music therapy itself.

In the last few years, there has been growing interest among creative and expressive arts therapists in general, to work toward theories which reflect the creative process of the arts in therapy. This interest to a large extent has been sparked through the lack of solid outcome research in psychotherapy, which is a school often embraced by music therapists seeking theoretical models.

Feder and Feder (1981) comment: "An increasing number of expressive arts therapists have begun to wonder aloud if...the expressive therapies should not develop independent theoretical structures (p. 53)."

This interest reflects the absence of well-grounded theory. True accountability cannot be satisfied by research methods finding their source in theories which do not address the essential elements of the experience of the creative process, a fundamental aspect of the Creative Arts therapies.

Music Therapy: The Theoretical Tradition

Despite this dearth, some theoretical fragments do exist in the field of music therapy. Historically, these works are discovered in conjunction with the development of training programs at the University of Kansas. As is often the case, such practical issues as training, the development of employment opportunities, and clinical practice are all inextricably linked with the design of theory.

One of the first training programs for music therapists in this country was established at the University of Kansas by music therapy pioneer, E. Thayer Gaston. His text *Music in Therapy* (1968), still serves as a basic text for some music therapy programs. Gaston's text was the first collection of works to portray music therapy as a field and thus greatly assisted the launching of music therapy as a profession.

This test can be viewed as a highly paradoxical work. The book is essentially an anthology of articles on practice. Gaston has very little to say about theory of music therapy and primarily embraces existing scientific theory in the form of behaviorism. Feder and Feder comment:

Despite Gaston's disavowal of dependence
on a particular psychological theory, an
examination of the specific programs
described in his collection and the research
included, reveals that operationally, the
majority are based squarely on behavioral
models. (p. 119)

A possible interpretation of the Gaston work is that
he had a sense of the theoretical movement, but was
torn between his belief in the *unique* potential of
music therapy and pressures to lay the groundwork
for accountable clinical practice and employment for
music therapy practitionners.

However, the seeds of music therapy theory are
contained in the Gaston text. One of the articles in
the anthology is entitled "Processes of Music
Therapy." This article was written by William Sears,
Gaston's colleague and successor at the University of
Kansas.

Within this article, Sears clearly establishes the
theoretical roots of music therapy in "process".

The Process of Music Therapy

Sears describes three classifications that underlie
the processes of music therapy: "1) experience within
structure; 2) experience in self-organization; 3)
experience in relating to others." (Gaston, p. 31)

On the theoretical level, Sears provides an
environmental approach—one which offers fields, conditions, relationships and self-organization. Explicit
within his three classifications are self-organization

and relationships (relating). Implicit are fields and conditions.

Operationally, this design breaks down in the dilemma of theoretical constructs versus pressures for outcome studies in the acceptable language of behaviorism—observable behavioral change.

For example, in his articulation of the experience of self-organization, Sears lists his elements of self-organization:

1)   Music provides self-expression;
2)   Music provides compensatory endeavors for the handicapped individual;
3)   Music provides opportunities for socially acceptable reward and non-reward;
4)   Music provides for the enhancement of pride in self. (p. 33)

Perhaps the most dramatic item in this list is item 3. This item was most readily accepted by advocates of behavioral research and reflects a significant development in the interface between what little theory this field had, clinical practice and outcome studies. This tendency toward behaviorism seems to be the result of a profession's need to survive and create accountability structures in a medical system, which at that time, generally avoided the aesthetic dimension, theories of self-organization, inner development, self-reliance and autonomy.

In addition, the Sears' list begs the question: Are "self-expression" and "socially acceptable" mutually compatible? This is characteristic of the Sears' style of ambiguity and paradox. In the final analysis, he stimulates more questions and engages his reader in a process of self-examination.

In Sears' own final analysis, he must have had a sense of the consequences of his creative expositions. This is reflected in the closing statements of his article on process:

> A theoretical formulation such as this may suffer one of several fates: It may pass into history having received little consideration. It may be examined and found wanting, but because of the study it required, result in a different, more adequate formulation of theory. Finally, it may prove of enough interest and worth to be put to the test in practice and research to be modified, improved and expanded. Hopefully, the latter fate will come to pass. In any case, processes in Music Therapy take place by *uniquely involving* (author's italics) the individual in experience within structure, experience in self-organization and experience in relating to others. (Gaston, p. 44)

Toward a Theory of Music Therapy

Shortly after the death of William Sears, New York University and the Musicians' Emergency Fund sponsored an International Symposium on Music Therapy, bringing together 36 music therapists, music psychologists and musicians from twenty countries around the world. Barbara Hesser, of New York University, organized this symposium and entitled the gathering: "Music in the Life of Man: Toward a Theory of Music Therapy."

After six days and nights of study groups, the Symposium members issued critical assessments on the State of the Art for the field of music therapy. One of the statements was:

> Music Therapy facilitates the creative process of moving towards wholeness by developing the ability and will to utilize the individual's potential for wellness in areas such as independence, freedom to change, adaptability, balance and integration. The implementation of Music Therapy involves interaction of the therapist, client and music. These interactions initiate and sustain musical and non-musical change processes which may or may not be observable. As the musical elements of rhythm, melody and harmony are elaborated across time, the therapist and client can develop existential relationships which optimize the quality of life. We believe Music Therapy makes a unique contribution to wellness because man's responsiveness to music is unique. (*Proceedings from the International Symposium on Music in the Life of Man*, 1982)

The New York group described music therapy as a "creative process," or more specifically the role of music therapy as a creative process. Even though Sears does not describe his processes specifically as "creative", the link between Sears' processes and the New York group is evident. Sears' phrase "experience within structure" is the key. For the music therapist, the structure of the music, the "musical elements", according to the New York group, is the guiding light of experience. Sears' approach conforms to the statement of the role of music therapy from the New York Symposium group. The symposium statement also notes the essential elements of relationships and self-organization. This is indicated in the following description; "As the musical elements of rhythm, melody and harmony are elaborated across time, the therapist and client can develop existential relationships which optimize the quality of life."

Within the structure of the musical experience, relationships develop—relationships to the music, relationships between client and therapist, relationships between sound, thought and feeling, etc. These relationships determine the "conditions" of the field of experience, actualized in music therapy as a field of sound and the human person. The interactions, determined and defined through conditions, which are created through the relationships, can "initiate and sustain musical and non-musical change processes...". Thus there is the implication of both conditions and fields.

Music therapy, according to Sears, creates a "unique involvement". The New York group goes further stating: "Music Therapy makes a unique contribution to wellness because man's responsiveness to music in unique."

William Sears created a significant piece of the theoretical picture, which would help to explore and define this uniqueness. The New York group expanded these fragments to include an even fuller architectural design.

An Environmental Approach: The Field of Sound

Sears introduced the concept of environment and implied a field of sound.

In the earliest stages of his work, Sears had developed five classifications of processes before refining these five into the three mentioned above. his original formulation was: "1) gratification; 2) structured experience; 3) environment conducive to recovery; 4) relationships; 5) diagnosis and evalua- tion." (p. 31)

In this earlier articulation, item three expresses Sears' explicit interest in the field/environment.

Bonny in some of her most current work uses the term "sound presence" and "envelope of sound" (private conversation). Bonny describes this phenom- enon as a safe container or field of sound in which people feel supported in the process of healing. In Bonny's view this supportive field guides the person into healthy change.

Bonny was, at one time, a member of the Gaston community. When it became clear that music therapy would be following the path of the behavioral sciences, Bonny broke with the general stream of development of music therapy and took her own research in the direction of consciousness and spirituality. The latest developments in the Bonny work represent her return to medicine and an integration of her consciousness studies into the medical context. Her "sound presence" is a system designed for hospitals, bringing her full circle back into medicine.

Bonny's "sound presence" and "envelope of sound" are similar to Sears' concept of "environment." Music provides a safe field for change, growth and recovery. Both Sears and Bonny are environmentalists, in this sense.

Other fragments of theory are available to support the concept of the field or environment in music therapy literature.

Kenny (1985) offers a description of such an "environment" in an article entitled: "Music: A Whole Systems Approach". Her context for practice is clinical musical improvisation.

> The time/space of musical improvisation is a synthesizing time and space in which a person is naturally drawn to give form and pattern through musical expression. There is randomness and waiting and receiving the authentic forms of human movement which are both mirrored and actualized through rhythm, melody, dynamics, etc.... The musical improvisation encourages a person to identify a pattern or way of organizing which has personal significance and meaning for the musicmaker. Within the improvisation, this field of being and acting in sound, ideas and feelings are allowed to float freely until the deep natural patterns emerge. In this way the Music Therapist creates an environment, a ritual space. (1985, p. 8)

In an earlier work, Kenny (1982) implies this same sort of field:

> Music is a resource pool. It contains many things—images, patterns, mood suggestions, textures, feelings, processes. If selected and used with respect and wisdom, the clients will hear what they need to hear in the music and use the ritual as a supportive context. (p. 5)

The Nordoff/Robbins techniques of musical improvisation are probably, as a group, one of the more accepted forms of music therapy. Although in their texts (1965, 1971, 1977) Nordoff and Robbins concentrate on descriptions of practice, focusing on musical form and ordering principles, they, too, imply an environment:

> Music can become something rare, evocative or consoling. It can become another landscape for him (the child in therapy), one in which he will be able to find more than the limits of his own being... It becomes a secure, fertile landscape of experience in which he feels himself quickened into communicative response—a new emotional stream begins to flow, nourishing a new awareness of self and of expressive capability. (1967, p. 56)

McMaster (1976), a practitioner of the Nordoff and Robbins techniques, also implies a creative process within a safe environment or field. Commenting on her work with emotionally disturbed children, she observed that the children learned the following in their musical improvisation experiences: "1) to stretch out past safe, familiar experiences; 2) to notice and value an expressive moment; 3) to invest concentration in an activity; 4) to sustain an enjoyable activity."

> This model affords a fluid role for the therapist, a framework which can include many different levels of participation, a creative and organic process stemming from and developing through the changing nature of its totality. (p. 6)

Her totality represents a field of experience in musical improvisation.

Boxill (1985) defines her work through the "continuum of awareness", borrowing from the Gestalt tradition, but still within the "field of sound." She describes this as a creative process which uses music functionally as a tool of consciousness to awaken, heighten and expand awareness of self, others and the environment. (p. 71)

Boxill sees this process of interaction with the environment (physiologically and psychologically) beginning with sensation. Her theoretical work finds its origin in her practice with the developmentally disabled. She describes music as a "tool of consciousness." Boxill defines music as structured tonal sound moving in time and space. (p. 5)

Organization and Self-organization

A large portion of the literature attempting to describe music therapy experience, and therefore at least moving in a theoretical direction, focuses on the tendency for music to encourage the human system to organize. Sears, the New York group, and others mentioned previously have emphasized the importance of structure and thus organization.

Given the behavioral orientation of many music therapy practitioners, this tendency toward "organization" often means that the therapist chooses music which will draw the patient into a particular type of organization which is "healthy". Relaxing music may calm a hyperactive child. Stimulating music may activate a depressed adult.

A considerable amount of research is now confirming that the human system does, in fact, adapt to sound input on both physical and psychological levels, i.e., a "sound presence", to borrow Bonny's term, does change the person.

One example of this research in the music therapy literature discusses the importance of "rhythmic entrainment". After describing his findings in a study exploring the relationship between music therapy and learning, Rider (1985) stated strongly that "rhythmic synchronization plays such an important role in learning that its function cannot be understated." (p. 19) Rider then proceeds to describe the possibility of matching the rhythmic synchronizations of the learner in order to initiate therapeutic change.

Rhythmic entrainment is often demonstrated in what music therapists call the "iso" principle, a term introduced by Altshuler in 1948 in an article entitled: "A Psychiatrist's Experience with Music as a therapeutic Agent." The "iso" principle instructs the music therapist to match the patient at the patient's own level of rhythm, melody, timbre, etc. It is assumed that if the patient sees that the therapist is willing to "entrain" with him, or join him in his sound representations, this willingness encourages the patient to be more open to explore and entrain with the therapist's rhythms, which ideally will reflect healthy patterns.

The "iso" principle conforms to the principles of organization, however, it is questionable in terms of "self-organization". This is a highly controversial issue among music therapists, and touches on questions of intervention versus the right to express, or even more specifically, "compliance versus expression".

As we have demonstrated, there seems to be a fundamental paradox about this issue in the music therapy culture-at-large. Sears stresses self-organization, yet operationally sets up an entrance for positive reinforcement for socially acceptable expression only.

Yet Sears still stated: "Experience in self-organizing concerns inner responses that may only be inferred from behavior and has to do with a person's attitudes, interests, values and appreciations, with his meaning to himself." (Gaston, p. 39)

Sears spoke of "inner responses", yet operationally, patients were rewarded only for "socially accepted responses" in the token economy.

The Dilemma of Uniqueness

The irony of the work of William Sears has to do with the clarity he expressed in terms of the creative process, the value of individual expression the accomodation to external systems. The field of music therapy, perhaps accomodated some of its own uniqueness in order to establish a foundation of acceptance for practice. However, in this process, perhaps some of the essential elements of music therapy were devalued, a result of the natural process of consensus. Creative process was one of those elements.

The context in which to observe and alter these accomodations emerges as the theoretical tendency of organization/self-organization.

Wheeler, a member of the New York Symposium, expresses this dilemma in her submission to the symposium papers:

> It seems that too often, Music Therapy researchers may have let the elements of individuality frighten us from even attempting to classify or categorize but that, crude though initial attempts may be, we must look for the relationships and explore them in a systematic manner. (*Proceedings from the International Symposium on Music in the Life of Man*, 1982, Wheeler, p. 1)

Wheeler exposes the dilemma—the fear of individuality—the link to the self-organizing system, and further, music therapy as a self-organizing system, as Kuhn's "community of professionals." Wheeler seeks the elements of the experience of music therapy, constituting a phenomenological approach, an eidic reduction. In her own theoretical language, she identifies three elements in music therapy:

> One is that people are variable; each person brings his or her own set of charac- teristics to the situation. The second ele- ment is that music is complex; a piece of music consists of different melodies, harmo- nies, rhythms, timbres, dynamics,etc. And third, the process of therapy means that, at any specific moment in therapy, certain things are brought to bear which are indi- vidual only to that moment. (*Proceedings from the International Symposium on Music in the Life of Man*, 1982, p. 1)

Summary

This exploratory review has studied some of the historical roots of the theoretical movement in the field of music therapy. There may not be a well-grounded, comprehensive theory. However, there are tendencies toward theory, which constitute seeds for theoretical growth in this field. Noted in this study are tendencies:

1) to consider music therapy as a creative process;

    2)   to imagine this process in a field;

    3)   to appreciate the significance of relation-ships in the field;

    4)   to appreciate the power of organization and self-organization in the musical experience;

    5)   to consider the conditions in the field.

If we are prepared to consider music therapy as a process-oriented art and science, we can thus identify four essential elements of the music therapy experience from this study of theoretical roots. These four elements are:

1) conditions;
2) fields or environments;
3) relationships;
4) organization/self-organization.

Perhaps the first is the least explored of the elements. Conditions are an important consideration in any field. What conditions does the therapist place into the field by being and acting who s/he is in the context of sound? There are many other questions about the condition factor. The sound expressions can be understood to express the conditions which help to define the field. It is important to consider these "conditions" even before the onset of the therapeutic relationship, since they may constitute non-verbal cues in the field. What conditions does the client bring into the field? Conditions represent strengths and limitations. Conditions determine what is accepted or rejected in the field.

Attention to the "field" is another significant factor. This is Bonny's "sound presence" and "envelope of sound", Sears' environment", Kenny's "resource pool" and Nordoff and Robbins' "landscape". This is the •container for change, the supportive context.

Both music and the human system are abstract and sensorial and both are relational systems. They operate in interplay with parts of their own system and with many other systems. This is the context for growth and change. Therefore it is critical to look into the aspect of "relationships" created in interplay between man and music.

The aspect of organization is equally significant. Organization is consistently a topic of theoretical concern among music therapists. Does the person organize the music or does the music organize the person? When and where is each appropriate?

Dialogue

Now that we have managed to discover some guideposts on the pathway to theory in music therapy, the question remains: What do we do with these bits of information?

The first task is to engage in critical analysis. It would be difficult to argue the point that music therapy is inherently a "creative" endeavor. We might observe practitioners who seem fixed or uncreative. We might feel rather uncreative ourselves at times.

Yet creativity lies deeply imbedded in the nature of our work.

Critical analysis enables us to keep this creative movement active. This analysis may take the form of asking questions, specifically questioning authority. In this case, the authority would be represented by those people who have articulated the bits of theory. Do we agree with their concepts, their language? Do their descriptions match our own unique experience of music therapy? Perhaps we can agree with some parts of their formulations and not others.

Comparison is another form of critique. Where do the theory-builders themselves agree and disagree? They are not all in one color, one shade, one hue, one thought. There is a vast spectrum of tone and color here.

A task which is sometimes difficult yet necessary in critical thinking is embracing paradox in order to explore the rich continuum between opposites.

Another important question: What is my world view? What are my assumptions? How do I see the world and thus my work through it? Certainly it will be more difficult to share a theory with someone whose worldview is diametrically opposed to ours. These differences become more finely-tuned when we get into the geometry of our experience. How do we shape our reality? How do we approach time and space? Are we oriented toward spatial considerations or temporal considerations, both, some of each, how much of each, when and where? An idiosyncratic term such as "time-ordered behavior" takes on a large perspective when it sifts through the layers of our experience into theory. What are the strengths and weaknesses of this kind of language in the "big picture?"

Each one of us brings his or her theory into each situation, each music therapy session, each class in techniques, each research design. Sometimes it is not necessary to articulate our theory. But it is essential to be aware of its development. Such awareness does not mean the theory is totally formed or understood. It means knowing that our theory is "in process", an alive and growing part of us, which has a direct influence on those whose lives we touch, especially our clients.

A handy tool for engaging in this process is the task of dialogue.

There is a dialogue between two sources. One source is the sum total of all the "others" who have engaged in the theory-building task—teachers, writers, researchers, colleagues, etc. The other source is you in your own direct experience of music therapy and your own unique interest in designing a foundation for yourself. This design may share a general pattern from the field of music therapy or not.

In either case, it is a representation of the uniqueness which is you.

A good way to engage in this contact with the source of self in the task of theory-building is to recall a particularly moving music therapy session with a client and to delve into your memory to the depth of that direct experience—the direct encounter between music and the human person in the form of the music therapy experience. This is your direct knowing, your direct source.

Then when you have felt this complete memory and you have felt its depth and its strength, play with trying to describe it to yourself or to friends or collegues in language which rings true to your experience. Through this play or improvisation with language, the dialogue between the two sources can begin.

If we give attention to this dialogue, each one of us and the field of music therapy as a whole may benefit. Some possible results are:

1. You feel more secure, in that you are developing a foundation for yourself.
2. The field of music therapy is more secure because music therapists are developing their unique formulations, thus securing the on-going creative construction of theory.
3. Our awareness of the abstract cycles back into practice. This may increase understanding enabling us to move on to another level of practice. In this way, our clients are served. This requires a commitment to an on-going dialogue in the relationship between theory and practice;
4. The field of music therapy remains in close contact with direct experience, not once or twice or three times removed;
5. We move forward in the creation of new language to describe our experience in music therapy.

Philosophy

Phenomenology is a revolution in man's understanding of himself and his world. But the newness and radicality of this revolution is faced with a problem, the same problem which arises in the epiphany of any new phenomenon. What phenomenology has to say must be made understandable—but what it has to say is such that it cannot be said easily in a language already sedemented and accomodated to a perspective quite different than that taken by the revolutionary. What eventually may be said must first be "sung". One only gradually learns to hear what sounds forth from the "song."
(From Don Idhe, *Sense and Significance*)

Why Philosophy?

If theory serves as a foundation for practice, philosophy serves as the foundation for theory.

Metaphorically we can imagine a philosophy as solid clear ground upon which to build our theoretical structures.

Philosophy asks questions of meaning.

Many of the disciplines which address human suffering tend to ignore the intimate connections between philosophy, theory and practice. Sometimes in the face of burning issues of human needs, our awareness of these necessary links is pushed aside for more practical considerations. Subsequently, over time, we are left with ungrounded architectural structures and techniques of practice without meaning.

Philosophy exists implicitly in each one of us, whether we acknowledge it or not and thus creates a condition, albeit non-verbal, of our engagement in experience.

There is a constant creative movement between philosophy, theory and practice which keeps a discipline and each individual in the discipline secure and capable of on-going change in the work. One springs out of the other. Each adjusts and learns from the others. There is a dialogue, an interaction between explicit and implicit forms.

The heart and soul of our philosophy and theory come forth to serve as the wellspring of our practice. The noticing, acknowledging and consistent developing of our philosophical base, as well as our theoretical structures, brings a fullness and security to our work as music therapists.

One of the dilemmas of the philosophical endeavor is that intimate, soulful and creative movements are sometimes difficult to remember because of the pressures of explicit activity. Yet our direct experience and the way we view it, in other words, our philosophy, have a direct connection. Our philosophy is the source and therefore the cause of many of our actions in our work. It informs our decisions.

And for the music therapist, as we have seen, the connection to direct experience is fundamental. In a sense we must be doing, or at least vividly remembering, music therapy experience while designing philosophy and theory. It seems important that we call forth every resource we know as "memory" of our moving moments with music and clients, while creating these more abstract formulations. In this way our architectural designs and our philosophical base are merely "remembering" the musical moments.

Our words mirror, if not replicate, our music therapy experience. We may think it rather strange to "play into" the philosophy and theory of science. But as music therapists that is what we do. We play a duet of music and the person.

In the walk between the worlds of art and science, this play must go on. It is a dance which will enable us each to find our place upon which to build.

As we are carving out our place in the larger picture of human development, how can we find a way of articulating a philosophy which honors our direct experience as music therapists? How can we find a method of inquiry into the nature of our work, which will keep us in the immediacy of our experience?

This exploration is a great adventure for each individual and music therapy as a whole.

We can look for allies on our way, explorers who have met the challenge of similar questions. These thoughts, insights and creations are like musical interludes, which guide or inspire us and help us to find a school in the philosophy and theory of science. We try a phrase here, a melodic pattern there. We add our own formulations, until as a whole, the composition resonates to that which seems true to our experience.

This is the journey into the philosophy and theory of science.

Philosophy and Theory of Science

If music can in fact be considered a language of immediacy, it seems obvious that any efforts in the design of language and construction of models describing the process of music therapy be closely connected to methods which keep us in touch with direct experience. In his work *Personal Knowledge*, Polanyi suggested a theory of knowledge based on a critical link to direct experience. In fact he claimed that we do not have knowledge outside of our experience. Thomas Kuhn in his seminal work *The Structure of Scientific Revolutions* used the term *paradigm* as a reference word for the design of models for science. His use of the term implies tacit knowing as one of the major resources for the design of all models of science. He spoke of these resources as "shared possessions of the members of a successful group" (p. 193). He proposed that the way to start sorting out and manifesting these shared possessions is by the presentation of exemplars within a particular field and the subsequent comparison in the perception of "known experience" of the phenomena represented in the exemplar. This way the convergent and divergent perceptions of a community of specialists will reveal themselves. This is the beginning of new paradigms. Kuhn stressed the importance of tacit knowledge and a type of community intuition which will eventually reveal similarities in thought.

Any research into the processes associated with music establishes a necessary link between art and science. Therefore research into the use of the arts would naturally be tinted with artistic reflection. Eisner made an interesting point in his comparison between scientific and artistic approaches to research when he claimed that any artistic approach to research is fundamentally associated with the discovery of meaning, not necessarily truth. He stressed the importance of the creation of images that people will find meaningful and from which their fallible and tentative views of the world can be altered, rejected or made more secure. Truth implies singularity and monopoly. Meaning implies relativism and diversity (1981, p. 9).

It seems sensible that an artistic researcher would be concerned with the "creation of images," which is the modus operandi of the world of art. The image is created subjectively by the artist and presented as an object to the audience as a reference, a measurement in the broad sense of the word, for alteration, rejection or validation of the perceiver's fallible and tentative views (Eisner). The dilemma is to find research attitudes and methods which utilize the sensibilities of both artist and scientist. This is particularly relevent in fields such as music therapy in which art forms represent the mode of being and acting. Research which is both artistic and scientific would be concerned with issues of both truth and meaning, objectivity and subjectivity.

Phenomenological Inquiry

The philosophy and theory of science which seems to suit this orientation to research into the creation of images is phenomenology.

Phenomenology is concerned with direct experience of a phenomenon. In its simplest form it is merely a tool for flooding "light" onto a phenomenon. It examines the appearances of things. Thus the phenomenological endeavor is one which focuses on perceiving, on seeing, illuminating.

Although the goal of phenomenology is one of description, on a more fundamental level, the task is to "reduce" all being to phenomenality (Husserl, 1965). The phenomenologists search for this phenomenality through the discovery of essences. Merleau-Ponty described phenomenology as the study of essences. For him, all problems amounted to finding definitions of essences. This discovery, he claims, puts essences back into existence. He saw all the efforts of phenomenology as being concentrated upon re-achieving a direct and primitive contact with the world, and endowing that contact with a philosophical status.

> It is the search for a philosophy which shall be a "rigorous science," but it also offers an account of space, time and the world as we 'live' them. It tries to give a direct descrip-tion of our experience as it is, without tak-ing account of its psychological origin and the causal explanations which the scientist, the historian, or the sociologist may be able to provide. (1973A, p. 357)

Thus, we have the phenomenological link to tacit knowledge, direct experience and being in the world.

Merleau-Ponty claimed that all knowledge of the world, even scientific knowledge, is gained from one's own particular point of view or from some experience of the world without which the symbols of science would be meaningless. He was concerned about the dissassociative results of science and believed that the modern task of philosophy and theory of science is to begin a reawakening of the basic experience of the world of which science is the second-order expression (1973, p. 73).

The phenomenological method carries this mandate. Through its link to direct experience it abandons the Cartesian mind-body split. It considers

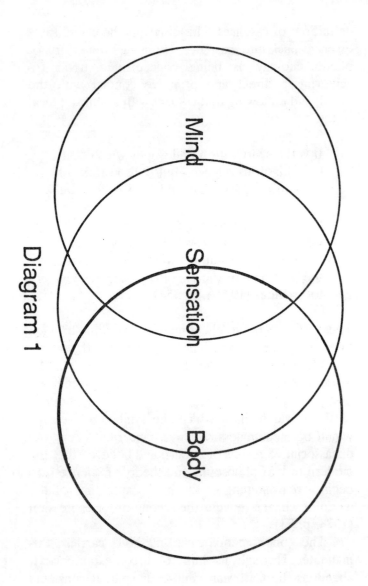

Diagram 1

perception as a critical tool in "viewing" and illuminating the world and of being in the world.

Existential Phenomenology

A study of the existential phenomenologists reveals a clear link not only to perception, but also to sensation. Although there is a distinction between thought or idea and sensation, both are equally important in viewing the world. Sensation is more closely associated with direct experience because of its physicality. Examples of sensations are colors, odors, tastes, sounds, tactual feelings, heat, cold, etc. (Grossman, 1984). This places the train of thought once again in the realm of art and the creation of image, whether in color, pattern, sound, form, etc. In fact, sensation may be the critical link in mind and body, because of its location in both. Sensations are experienced sensorily, in the body, whether these are subtle or gross sensations. Sensation is how we gather information about the world. It is direct experience. It also translates into mental constructs such as perceptions and thought forms as well as feelings. With this in mind we could consider sensation as an integrative force connecting mind and body (see figure 1 on page 52).

Herbert Marcuse took another step, bringing phenomenology even further into the realm of art when he established the link between perception, sensation, phantasy, imagination and knowledge.

Marcuse also added the dimension of the global, mythic reality.

> The truths of the imagination are first realized when phantasy itself takes form, when it creates a universe of perception and comprehension—a subjective and at the same time objective universe. This occurs in art. The analysis of the cognitive function of phantasy is thus led to aesthetics as the "science of beauty": behind the aesthetic form lies the repressed harmony of sensuousness and reason. (1962, p. 130)

Marcuse was concerned with the development of the seemingly paradoxical "science of beauty," a universe of perception and comprehension which is both subjective and objective. He spoke of the repressed harmony between sensuousness and reason.

He sought to undo the repression through the aesthetic dimension and to demonstrate the inner connection between pleasure, sensuousness, beauty, truth, art, function and freedom.

Consciousness

Having established the fundamental link to direct, and what we might now call, *sense* experience we can consider the next significant point of phenomenology, i.e., consciousness. So important is the issue of consiousness that Grossman defined phenomenology as the study of the essence of consciousness (p. 144). We can assume that this is not a consciousness which represents pure abstract thought, but one which incorporates direct experience as its source. So phenomenology consists of a reflection on consciousness, or ordinary mental acts of perception, experience, desire, fear, etc. He considered the subject matter of phenomenology to be consciousness itself (p. 144).

It is important to remember that at its core phenomenology is a transcendent philosophy, dedicated to the elevation of consciousness. Grossman reflected on the paradox and exquisite beauty of the philosophy when he said:

> There is the act itself and then there is its object. Beyond these noemata, transcending them, lies the non-mental world. This world is forever beyond the direct grasp of consciousness. Both the self and the world are beyond our reach. But in the middle, between the two, dwells consciousness in splendid lucidity. (p. 146)

In the aesthetic dimension, our senses are stimulated by sound, color, pattern texture, etc. Through the senses, we perceive *beauty* and the doors of perception open into the development of consciousness. Thus there is an intimate link between sensation and consciousness, the space between self and world. In the world of human development and healing, consciousness is the gateway to change.

In this figure (see figure 2 on page 57), the new element is *consciousness,* now joined to *sensation.* This link liberates consciousness from the realm of the abstract and expands it to include the world of concrete experience or sensation. There is an interaction between sensation and consciousness between the physical and the mental, which can trigger awareness, growth and change. One of the possible limitations of the cognitive and verbal psychologies is the abstraction created by the separation from the world of concrete experience through solely intellectual and verbal abstraction. This figure has as a primary aspect the fundamental aspect of the arts–*sensation.* Thus we see Marcuse's ideal of a science of beauty with the marriage of sensation and the realm of abstract thought in the form of reason. If this link can be assumed we clearly realize the relationship between the sensation of art (in this case music) and the development of consciousness.

The Phenomenological Method

The phenomenological method has to do with the discovery of essences in some form of description. Very often this is demonstrated in detailed descriptions of the concrete events, situations, behaviors of a particular phenomenon. However, the method also provides for more than the elucidation of concrete events and observations. And in this more subtle form of perception we see an entrance for the artistic view.

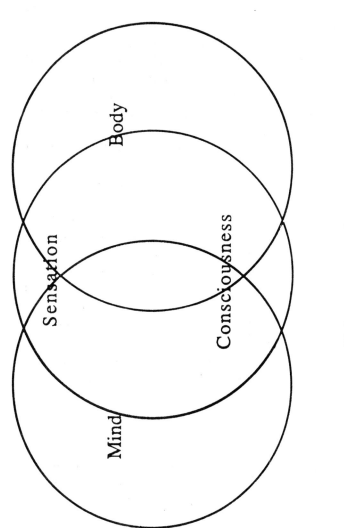

Diagram 2

The method of the phenomenological endeavor is called *eidic reduction*, or the search for essences. These essences are considered links to direct experience rather than universals (Grossman, p. 138). However, essences are not always easily observed through concrete data. The method provides a particular vehicle for the vision or conceptualization of experience, as observed and perceived in the realm of abstract thought about direct experience. This still conforms to Husserl's concept of the "bracketing of the objective world", by providing a framework through which to perceive concrete reality.

The task is always to locate *phenomenality*. Edmund Husserl, the founder of phenomenology, introduced a vehicle whose purpose is to determine the essences of a phenomenon through what he called "free phantasy variation." It is neither purely inductive (empirical) nor deductive (as is formal logic), but involves the use of intuition. Here "phantasy" retains the "ph" of the German *phantasie* to emphasize its relation to the Greek root *phaino*—meaning "to bring to the light of day," from which *phenomenology* is derived. The heart of this method is examining various possibilities of what may be examples, picture or images of the phenomenon in order to determiine what are its essential elements. These variations need not be restricted to the factual or the possible, but may be purely imaginative, or represent pure perception on the part of the observer (Hegel, 1977; Husserl, 1965).

Importance of Hermeneutics

A particular area of phenomenological research pertinent to the creative arts therapies is hermeneutics, the science of interpretation. The central theme of hermeneutics, as explained by Heidegger is "the modes of engagement." For Heidegger, the primary mode of engagement is the "ready-to-hand" mode, which once again demonstrates the phenomenological commitment to direct experience.

> When we carry out activities, our awareness is essentially holistic. We are aware of the situation we find ourselves in, not as an arrangement of discrete physical objects and not as a portion of the physical universe, but globally, as a whole network of interrelated projects, possible tasks, thwarted potentialities, and so forth. This network is not laid out explicitly, but it is present as a "background" to the project we are concerned with, and we can turn to aspects of the network and bring them into focus. There is no deliberate means-end framework. (Packer, 1985, p. 1083)

Hermeneutics supposes that it is through reflection on this gestalt that we interpret our experience—always keeping an eye out for the whole, yet in direct relation to experience, e.g., in the "ready-to-hand" mode. The hermeneutic science assumes that one cannot understand a particular act

without understanding the context in which it
occurs—a systems principle.

The ready-to-hand mode involves a complexly
woven network that Heidegger called the referential
totality (Packer, p. 1086). This referential totality in
a sense is the ongoing source of our knowing, serving
as a constant reference point to our direct
experience.

The particular structure of a hermeneutic
characterization is a semantic one, not a logical or
causal one. Its relationships are meaningful ones,
sensible and necessary; but only in terms of the
particular historical and cultural situation under
investigation (Packer, p. 1089).

Heuristic Inquiry

Another aspect of phenomenological study which
seems relevent is the heuristic approach. This
particular approach mirrors the goals of the general
phenomenological inquiry, e.g., a search for the
discovery of meaning and essence in significant
human experience. It also seeks the disclosure of
truth. Its unique aspects have to do with a belief that
self-experience is the most important guideline in the
pursuit of knowledge. Once again, this has to do with
the link to tacit knowledge and direct experience.
One only knows what one has experienced in the
self. The refreshing quality of this line of method-
ological thinking is the importance of the researcher
in the process of the study. Any research project can
be considered a design of the researcher's world view,

or some aspect of that view, because one can only create out of what one knows to be true and meaningful in the self, then in relation to the world.

Douglass and Moustakas (1985) presented a three-phase model representing the steps of heuristic inquiry:

1) Immersion (exploration of the question, problem or theme)
    Indwelling
    Internal frame of reference
    Self-search
2) Acquisition (collection of data)
    Tacit knowing
    Intuition
    Inference
    Self-dialogue
    Self-disclosure
    Significant-symbolic representation
3) Realization (synthesis)
    Intentionality
    Verification
    Dissemination (1985, pp. 45-6)

Their general description of this mode of inquiry rings of the creative process:

It is difficult to describe the heartbeat of heuristic inquiry in words alone—so much of the process lurks in the tacit dimension, in mystery, in the wild promptings of imagination, and in edgings of subtlety. Heuristics encourages the researcher to go wide open and to pursue an original path that has its origins within the self and that discovers its direction and meaning within the self. It does not aim to produce experts who learn the rules and mechanics of science; rather, it guides human beings in the process of asking questions about phenomena that disturb and challenge their own existence. (p. 53)

Systems

As organized sound, music itself is a system. A school of philosophical and theoretical thought which assists us in our model-making is Systems Thinking. The most basic attempt of the systems theorist is the design of models which help us to understand and thus manage energy.

One of the major orientations of the systems thinkers is their wholehearted acceptance of the challenge to view the universe not as a collection of physical objects but rather as a complicated web of relations between the various parts of a unified whole (Wilbur, 1982). This, too, sounds like music.

In this sense systems thinking is always a global concern. According to Wilbur this shift in the scientific spectrum has to do with the entrance of quantum theory. Thus in modern physics the fields become primary, as opposed to Newtonian physics, in which forces arose from separate material bodies (Sheldrake, 1986.)

Lazlo (1972) saw this movement as a shift toward rigorous but holistic theories. This means a view of facts and events within the context of wholes, forming integrated sets with their own properties and relationships. Looking at the world in terms of sets of integrated relations constitutes the systems view.

Nature is the constant grounding for the systems perspective. The view of nature and man is nonanthropocentric, but it is not nonhumanistic.

> [systems] are goal-oriented, self-maintaining, and self-creating expressions of nature's penchant for order and adjustment. Seeing himself as a connecting link in a complex natural hierarchy cancels man's anthropocentrism, but seeing the hierarchy itself as an expression of self-ordering and self-creating nature bolsters his self-esteem and encourages his humanism. (Laszlo, 1972B, p. 118)

Thus systems thinking is a vehicle for man to appreciate and define his link to nature, and to use that vision as a constant reference point in the design of natural structures for any human event.

A system is basically a scheme or structure. Eliade considered fruitful structuralism the kind in which one is constantly asking oneself about the essence of a set of phenomena and about the primordial order that is the basis of their meaning. (Eliade 1963) He thus articulated the link between phenomenology and systems.

Whole systems theorist, Jose Argüelles sought the primordial order suggested by Eliade (Argüelles 1985). Argüelles contended that we have lost the sense of the natural order through a state of *holonomic amnesia*. He defined this amnesia as a state of forgetfulness of the primordial order, the order which existed before technological advance. He claimed that this sense can be recovered only through allowing our consciousness to travel through what he called *aboriginal continuity*, an intuitive level of awareness which retains the sense and structure of the primordial order and which is a necessary and critical compliment to the *civilzation advance*, which reflects our logical and technological knowings. According to Argüelles, it is only through curing our holonomic amnesia that we can in fact know and apply the primordial order, the natural order which is reflected in nature.

He proposed a model of unified field theory, as a universal resonant mechanism. He furthur believed that there is a critical need at this point in time for what he called holonomic reciprocity, a type of interaction between subsets which unifies them through an understanding of a unifying principle or law. This requires acknowledging our mutual resonance and interdependence, as well as interactive components of our systems. The importance of an awareness of the reality and details of resonating fields is the key to Argüelles' thought. He believed the only way to accomplish this awareness is a sincere unified effort between aboriginal continuity and civilzation advance.

Argüelles saw science as representing the mode of civilization advance (CA) and art as representing the mode of aboriginal continuity (AC) and attached great importance to the activities of art and creative process in order to do away with holonomic amnesia.

The Field

Field theory is a category of systems thinking. McWhinney (1984) described some of the discrete characteristics of the field thinkers. Field thinkers carry the imprint of the holonomic design from the general systems tradition. However, their discrete characteristics have to do with their tendency to view boundaries as unnatural, and as mere assumptions created for the convenience of understanding and articulation. Since the field theorists consider the field infinite in many aspects, only aspects of it can be described and their influence articulated at any point in time and space.

> A field theory describes the ways in which forces are resolved, that is, how the impact of the various forces continually balance out and what paths a system follows in its response to those forces. The formal statements in field theories are about the distribution of conditions, qualities, or forces over certain dimensions. (McWhinney 1989, p. 54)

Field thinking represents the position of

maximum interdependence among elements. The field is always an environment in which any point can represent the whole, through the vision of an organic creative process. The field theory is expressed in formative terms, that is, in terms of patterns, relations, ratios as opposed to numbers and processes as opposed to objects affecting each other.

Field thinking was not easily accepted in the world of science. McWhinney considered the cultural trends of the tumultuous decade of 1965-1974 as the starting place for acceptance and support of the field approach. He named the following movements as critical to this change in the scientific climate:

1) the growing awareness of Eastern thinking (D. T. Suzuki and Alan Watts),
2) the rebellion against allopathic medicine and the emergence of holistic approaches to health,
3) discontent with the prevailing theories of evolution,
4) the emergence of the "third-force" psychologies and their use in the understanding and design of work,
5) the existential psychologies of Peter Marcuse, Norman O. Brown, Martin Buber and others,
6) the rising awareness of danger to the ecology from human excesses (Rachel Carson),
7) the invention of the laser through which the holographic ideas (founded in the late 1940's) were made practical,

8) and, perhaps more important and more subtle, an involvement with self-awareness which, while exaggerated in the excesses of the "me generation," has now emerged as a deep engagement with *consciousness*. (1989, p. 62)

In general, support for field thinking came from concern with biological phenomena, the sense of unity of man with the ecology and the sense of the deep interrelatedness of the elements of a living oraganism—particularly human.

In the 1940's and 1950's Kurt Lewin attempted to design field theories for social science, including social systems and the dynamics of personality. But his work was not generally accepted and applied due to the climate of the psychological sciences. Yet he offers a comprehensive theory and praxis of field thinking. He maintained the environmental perspective and designed concepts such a personal life space, representing spatial configurations over time around the individual and various social structures (Lewin 1935).

He stressed the interdependence of parts, the links to Gestalt psychology, the establishment of pathways which create interconnecting networks in the spaces of personality and group.

Dialogue

The school of phenomenology keeps us in touch with our direct experience. It seeks to describe the essence of our experience. Polanyi, Marcuse and Merleau-Ponty allow us our firm footing in the world of art, yet offer us a bridge into the world of science. We are supported by logical and intuitive modes. We have our sound sensation. We have our imagination. Through free phantasy variation, our sense and sight of the subtle can assist us in the design of theory.

Systems thinkers offer the global perspective. This philosophy magnifies the unifying principles of our discipline, the organizational aspects of sound in music. With the field thinkers, we find an ecological approach to sound. They also offer us process, conditions and relationships. Argüelles offers art as a connecting tissue, a touchstone to our ancient roots.

What is your philosophical ground?

Can you place yourself in a philosophical tradition?

Would you create an entirely new philosophical stance?

Do you consider yourself existential or time-bound?

Do you identify more with information received directly through the senses or do you like it better when there is a more well-defined abstract form to work from?

Do you have a method in self-study, in work-study?

Do you believe in consciousness?

Which do you prefer: the closer territory of consciousness or the far reaches of consciousness?

Do you believe that your images have an impact on the way you organize your reality and function in the world?

Do you feel better in your logical mode or your intuitive mode, or do you like a combination of both and when and how much?

Do you seek truth or beauty or do you believe that they are the same in one?

Where would you place music therapy in the philosophy and theory of science or does it belong there at all?

Do you agree or disagree with Merleau-Ponty, Marcuse, Argüelles?

Would you pursue more information about their ideas?

These are only a few questions to start you off. You might try the inner dialogue, two parts of yourself, perhaps the artist and the scientist. Or you may have a dialogue between the whole of you and the outside consensus. Or you may dialogue with a friend, particularly a friend interested in the same topic, maybe a colleague, another music therapist.

Chapter four

The Field of Play

Essential Elements of the Music Therapy Experience

Psychotherapy takes place in the overlap of two areas of playing, that of the patient and that of the therapist. Psychotherapy has to do with two people playing together. The corollary of this is that where playing is not possible then the work done by the therapist is directed towards bringing the patient from a state of not being able to play into a state of being able to play.
(From D. W. Winnecott, *Playing and Reality*)

Essential Elements of the Music Therapy Experience

Introduction: The Field

What is a "field"?

The term "field" brings to mind a concentrated area of earth covered with delicate yellow and white flowers called daisies or an alpine meadow surrounded by snow-capped peaks. It also brings to mind an empty, clear brownish or greenish area of earth surrounded by trees—a *field of play*. Instead of flowers this particular field will hold humans who seem to move a bit like flowers. The two differences are that they are usually kicking or chasing a round object about on this field and second, they are not rooted to the earth. This makes them freer to move about than flowers.

This mixed freedom allows humans to engage in other fields—fields of awareness, fields of study, fields of thought.

An entire field of thought has developed around and about our curiousity about "the fields," whether we are a physicist, a football coach, a child looking for deer, whatever. There must be something reassuring about the idea of being in a field—whatever its constitution. Perhaps we remember something which pulls us back to that type of space. A field seems to be a reasonable way to perceive or imagine reality. If we can imagine that boundaries contain a space, we are not bombarded by sensory and psychic stimuli. The concept of "the field" allows us to focus and appreciate that which is in the field, and the conditions and relationships among the participants contained within this space.

The term "condition" is a bit of a hard pill to swallow most of the time.

For example, we seek "unconditional" love.

I suppose a safe way to approach the topic is to find a point of agreement.

We are all in the human condition.

Who would deny that?

This condition can be used as we choose. It brings us home to paradox.

We are prisoners of our conditions—limited and bound. Yet conditions are also paradoxically what allow us to grow, expand and change.

Many people believe that there is a certain beauty in the human condition and all the conditions which accumulate to create the human condition.

After all, "beauty", has a rather broad definition when it comes to the "human ondition." It contains even suffering, pain, loss. This is the ebb and flow of human life—love and loss, suffering and joy, pain and pleasure, and on and on.

The Navaho help. The goal of Navaho life is to "walk in beauty". One of their daily prayers:

> With beauty before me, I walk
> With beauty behind me, I walk
> With beauty above me, I walk
> With beauty below me, I walk
> From the East beauty has been restored
> From the South beauty has been restored
> From the West beauty has been restored
> From the North beauty has been restored
> From the zenith in the sky beauty has been restored
> From the nadir of the earth beauty has been restored
> From all around me beauty has been restored.
> (Witherspoon, pp. 153-4)

They describe a field of beauty which surrounds the human person.

For music therapy it is a natural association. For "music", is in the aesthetic domain, and restoration, rehabilation and re-creation are our task.

So conditions exist—and they are part of the beauty.

The human person—the client or the therapist—is a field full of conditions—an environment—similar to the alpine meadow, the swamp, the prairie, and full of beauty, surrounded by beauty.

We can say that the client, being a field of beauty, is whole and complete, unique, an aesthetic. In a sense, the process of development is to expand this field through increasing or decreasing certain conditions, or merely re-organizing or creating new patterns of conditions.

A great deal of thought has been put into the organizing aspect of this field.

But let's fall back a bit into the undifferentiated field of beauty—no patterns, no sound, no organization—pure and undefined, vast, full of potential, hope, creativity.

Primary Elements or Fields

The aesthetic (blue)

> *Definition*: The *aesthetic* is a field of beauty which is the human person. This field contains all non-verbal cues, which are communicated by the individual in being and acting and are perceived through the intuitive function. The *aesthetic* is an environment in which the conditions include the individual's human tendencies, values, attitudes, life experience and all factors which unite to create the whole and complete form of beauty, which is the person. Furthermore, each therapist and client is a complete and whole aesthetic. In and through the aesthetic domain, we

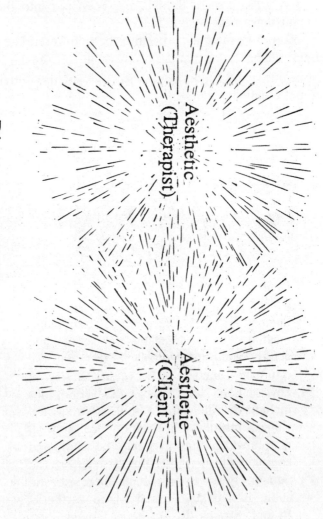

Diagram 3: The Aesthetics

express our human conditions. The task of the therapist is to honor and notice the conditions in the field of the client. The aesthetic of the therapist is significant and highly formative in the interplay which will come out of the mutual sharing of space because the therapist, essentially, invites the client into the broader *field of play.* Her conditions set the tone, and in a sense, determine that which is accepted and rejected as being and acting in the mutual field-to-be-created in the relationship between therapist and client. By nature, the aesthetic is open and expanding, always available for input. (See figure 3 on page 76.)

Principles of the aesthetic:

1) An *aesthetic* represents that which one carries and communicates into the world based on the screening system of choices and judgements regarding that which one considers to be "beautiful." (Assumption: As one moves toward beauty, one moves toward wholeness, or the fullest potential of what one can be in the world.)

2) An *aesthetic* represents the conditions one establishes by "being one who is" in relation to self and others.

3) In the therapeutic situation, the therapist is dominant in the field because the therapist essentially invites a client into her field to engage in actions designed by the therapist. Since expression is a creative force, the action actualizes the *aesthetic*. Therefore, her conditions are highly formative in the new field-to-be-created from the relationship between the aesthetic and the next primary field, the *musical space*. The therapist will attempt to equalize conditions through imitation and modeling of the patient's sound forms. This also serves to educate the therapist about the aesthetic of the patient, to learn, to grow, and to expand.

So, therapist and client are each a whole and complete, vibrating, rich, energy form, full of potential. This form or field is experienced on the intuitive level by both therapist and client before the onset of "therapy", before the first word, the first sound. It is a kind of encounter in what we might call pre-sound. Yet it is a time for gathering significant information for the new field-to-be-created through mutual participation in sound creation.

What does the music therapist do initially?
The music therapist provides the conditions for the establishment of a *musical space*.

The musical space (violet)

Definition: The *musical space* is a contained space. It is an intimate and private field created in the relationship between the therapist and client. It is a sacred space, a safe space, which becomes identified as "home base," a territory which is well known and secure. In early childhood development, it is similar to the space created between mother and child. Trauma necessitates the recovery of such a space for growth and change. It is a time when a person must reorganize and reintegrate him/herself, after trauma, a break in natural and healthy development. Initial entry into this space is gained when participants are motivated to make the first "sound," a creative gesture, a risk, a self-motivated action from an intention to engage. In a sense, the space is "sealed off" or contained, when both participants have joined each other in these first sounds. They get to know each other in the territory. In this field of musical being and acting, the emerging process of delicate new beginnings in development is enacted in musical form. (See figure 4 on page 81.)

Principles in the Musical Space:

1) The *musical space* has its source in the aesthetics of the client and the therapist. It is that space or field or environment which is created through mutual intention and first action (engagement). It is a closed space, an intimate space based on the relationship between therapist and client.

2) This origin represents the conception of relationship in a musical field, as well as relationships in all that is represented in the musical form (feelings, thoughts, sensations, behaviors).

3) This is sacred space because of the nature of its origins and represents a delicate and powerful moment in time. It is the first time something new comes into being and indicates a receptivity to creation (change) and thus to resources in the contained field of the *musical space* difined through the relationship between therapist and client.

4) When the two *aesthetics* of therapist and client merge, enough trust will develop to create a new field which through the musical play and expansion of the closed field, given the proper conditions, grows and expands into the *field of play*.

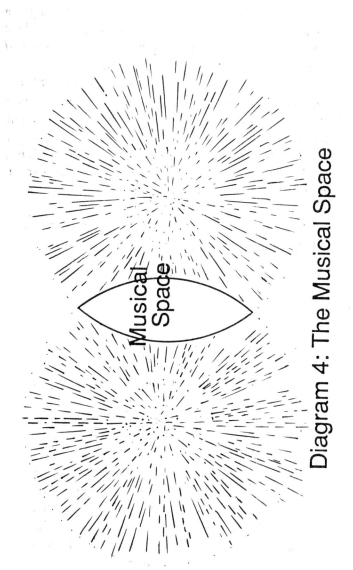

Diagram 4: The Musical Space

So the *musical space* is created through a magnetic pull. That which can come together does come together to create a new field in the *musical space*.

After trust is established and the participants are familiar with the conditions in home base—perhaps expressed through a recurring melodic or rhythmic form, a particular tonality or dynamic, they *know* each other and there is security and confidence enough to initiate a sense of play and experimentation.

At some point this experimentation bursts into an open space—*the field of play*.

The field of play (red)

Definition: The *field of play* (see figure 5 on page 83) is a space of experimentation, modeling, imitation in sound forms which express, represent and communicate significant feelings, thoughts, attitudes, values, behavioral orientations, issues of growth and change. It is an open and expanding field and occurs only after safety has been established in the *musical space*. It has the quality of "surprise", playfulness, fluidity and

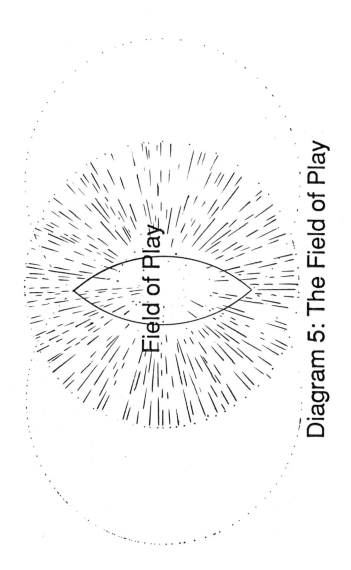

Field of Play

Diagram 5: The Field of Play

confidence. It is analogous to the stage of
human development in which the secure
infant reaches out into the world, traveling
beyond the mutual space shared with mother to experiment with the world outside the
mother/child relationship.

Principles of the field of play:

1) The *field of play* has its source in the
musical space and expands into an open
field which incorporates four secondary
fields: *ritual*, *a particular state of consciousness*, *power*, and *creative process*.

2) This field anticipates the movement of
the self-organizing system, which naturally
moves toward wholeness and expansion,
given the strengths and limitations of the
conditions in the field. Representational
sound forms, or responses to sounds,
emerge which both reflect and create this
movement and change. This process is
constantly supported through the continuing
awareness of the relationships established in
the *musical space*, and the randomly experienced sense of beauty in the conditions of
the *field of the aesthetic*. This awareness
provides the option of returning periodically
to a field of security, or one lacking
definition. There is a new found freedom

here to play and expand into experimental
forms offered in requisite variety, through
memory and action, from the undifferentiated, unpatterned, and open *aesthetic*.

3) This is multidimensional, expansive,
dynamic play in a field of expressive sound
forms yielding a creative process.

So we play and fold in and fold out of the
musical texture. We scout new territory—new sound
forms, which represent and express and create new
ways of being.

Whereas the *musical space* and the *field of play*
draw partially from concepts described in related
fields of psychology and human development the
element of *field of play* initiates relationships into
secondary elements which represent ancient healing
systems: *ritual, a particular state of consciousness,
power* and *creative process*, the last of which brings
us full circle into contemporary issues of healing and
therapy. (See figure 6 on page 87.)

Secondary Elements or Fields

Ritual (green)

> *Definition*: *Ritual* has a sacred quality, just as the *musical space*. It too, is contained. It also serves as home base. It is an arena of repeatable forms and gestures, the constants, which provide a ground base for innovation. *Ritual*, in musical improvisation, constitutes sounds and behaviors which are repeated over the course of the session. *Ritual* interplays with a particular state of consciousness to create a feeling of existential time, so that all which can emerge, does emerge, given the conditions in the field, within the time of the session.

In ancient times rituals triggered trance states, a state of being in which to fly—to gather, to journey. The repeatable forms in music, serve as rituals which can also initiate a sense of flight. They can alter brain waves and chemistry. They can, aesthetically, create a homebase, a sense of security, so that one can feel safe enough to fly into a *particular state of consciousness*.

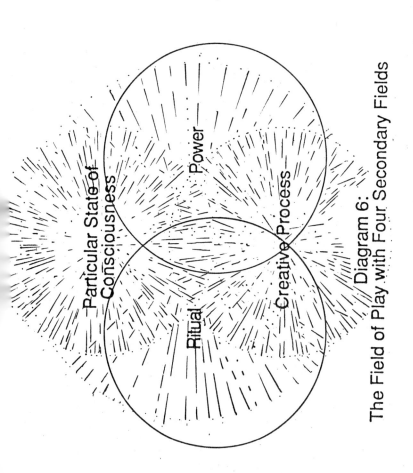

Diagram 6:
The Field of Play with Four Secondary Fields

A particular state of consciousness (dark blue)

> *Definition*: The *particular state of consciousness* opens the fields to more input. It is a state of deep concentration and focused attention, yet deep relaxation. It allows a receptivity to new experience, new forms, new sound perceptions in the movement toward wholeness.

When one flies in the sound, a feeling of inner motivation can develop—an embodiment of newness, growth, *power*.

Power (orange)

> *Definition*: *Power* is that cumulative energy which draws one into new possibilities in the arena of change. *Power* is experienced through a dialogue between inner motivation, strength and movement and significant external resources in the existent field. Because of its need to accumulate energy, *power* is enacted through contact with threshold points. Therefore it necessitates a containment for the accumulation of energy, which can then burst forth into experimentation for growth and change.

When one feels powerful, one has the courage to engage in creative process—to search in the vastness as well as the hidden recesses for the "right" sound in the process of creative self-organization.

Creative process (rose)

> *Definition*: The *creative process* is the interplay of forms, gestures and relationships, which as a whole constitute the context for a movement toward wholeness. It is an existential being and acting which is not product-oriented and which appreciates each emerging moment as the only moment in time, yet acknowledges the past with attention for possible future movement. It is informed by love, the intelligence of the heart, and thus the knowledge of the self-organizing system. It assumes that given its creativity, a safe environment and appropriate resources, after trauma, a person will naturally use the creative process to facilitate reorganization and re-integration. The process is the product.

The Field of Play: The Holographic Model

(See the colored plate which faces page 90.)

Discussion of the Holographic Model

The holographic paradigm informs us that the brain is a hologram perceiving and participating in a holographic universe. (Wilber, p. 3)

> Our brain mathematically constructs "concrete" reality by interpreting frequencies from another dimension, a realm of meaningful, patterned primary reality that transcends time and space. The brain is a hologram, interpreting a holographic universe. (Wilber, p. 5)

We can imagine the music therapy experience to be a reflection of the holographic universe as well as an essential part of that holographic universe. The *Field of Play* holographic model provides a visual description of this process as it interplays through the course of a music therapy experience.

We see the opening and closing nature of the model, in each of the fields, which alternate between opening and closing, reflecting the movement of nature itself. The elements of *musical space*, *ritual* and *power* are contained visually within strict boundaries. The elements of the *aesthetic*, the *field of play*, a particular *state of consciousness*, and the *creative process* are open and expanding forms.

One of the frustrations of presenting such a holographic model on a flat surface, is that it is virtually impossible to accurately depict the multi-dimensional aspects of the process. This is particularly true with the third element, the *Field of Play*.

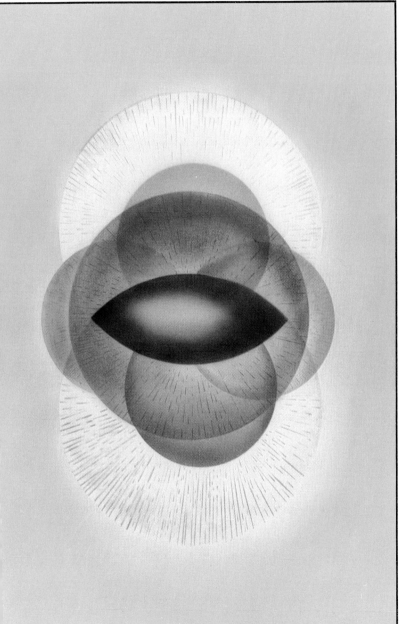

It may be a stage process. Yet each element is essential and continues to be so. Conditions may change: some are retained, some are discarded in the play, informed by the requirements of the creative process. The so-called goal, the creative process, which in actuality is manifesting itself from the onset, and merely developing over time, reaches an intense level of complexity by the end, which has initiated beginnings and endings of simultaneous processes, which are impossible to picture on a one-dimensional surface.

As indicated in chapter two, this particular model was designed to incorporate the established essential elements identified within the theoretical tradition of music therapy. These essential elements were discovered after an investigation of the work of William Sears, Helen Bonny, previous Kenny work and other theoretical fragments from several music therapy practitioners.

Thus the elements of the music therapy tradition form the basis for the *Field of Play*, which expands the elements in light of the clinical work of Kenny, observed through the phenomenological method.

Yet the four elements identified by Sears appear in all seven of the essential elements described in the *Field of Play*. All four elements of conditions, fields, relationships and organization are contained in all seven elements of the *Field of Play*.

For example, the *aesthetic* has conditions, is a field, forms relationships and is by nature in relationship and participates in organization, as essential elements of its existing and functioning. The same is true for *musical space*, etc.

The aspect of organization which is developed here is the result of the formation of "relationships", one important aspect shared by both man and music.

Certainly, as mentioned in chapter two, there has been a great emphasis on the aspect of organization in previous theoretical and practical work in music therapy. The focus on other areas here has been a response to the deficit of information on other aspects of the music therapy experience. An overemphasis on organization has often resulted in detailed analysis of musical form and human behavior, as opposed to the more general feeling texture of the music, attention to the aesthetic domain, which gives a particular perceptual orientation toward "conditions."

Narrative Description of the Field of Play

In this model all seven essential elements are described as fields. Each field provides an environment with conditions. When fields overlap or come together, they form a relationship between fields which then creates new fields. The dynamic component of the model is thus relationships between fields, and more specifically conditions in the fields expressed in musical form.

The first three fields can be considered stages in time although not necessarily chronological time.

1) The *aesthetic*
2) The *musical space*
3) The *field of play*

They are primary fields.

The last four fields are contained in the *field of play* and represent a four-fold interactive set. They are not necessarily time-ordered and are determined more through personal tendencies, cultural orientation and comfort of style.

The four secondary fields, contained in the third primary *field of play* are:

1) *Ritual*
2) *Particular state of consciousness*
3) *Power*
4) *Creative process*

Emphasis is on the continuity of fields as energy continues to move, whether fields are open or contained. They proceed organically. Also, although there are stages in time, there is not a hierarchical value placed on one field over another. All are essential and of equal value. The music therapist strives to attain the third primary element, the *field of play*, because it is a space with maximum growth potential. However, if other previous fields are forgotten, the high energy of the *field of play* is minimized. Therefore the music therapists is challenged to constantly be aware of the essential nature of all seven fields simultaneously.

It is not a linear process, but rather multi-dimensional. Relationships multiply exponentially. There are relationships between all the fields which are not described here.

For example, because the fields grow in number without discarding previous fields (although conditions are discarded), there is a relationship between the *aesthetic* and *power*. There are also multiple relationships between all the various elements, e.g., *musical space*, *field of play*, *ritual*, *creative process*. Creative relationships create more relationships.

It would be virtually impossible to name all the conditions establishing a field. Within this framework, an attempt is made to emphasize the importance of acknowledging conditions. This is particularly true in the initial stages, when the aesthetic of the therapist is a powerful field, which either supports or inhibits the patient's attempts at growth through establishing conditions by her way of being and acting within the context of the music therapy session. Some examples of conditions in the seven fields are:

1) Conditions in the field of the *aesthetic*:

  —value for beauty in changing places of human development
  —love
  —anticipation
  —existential attitude
  —value for the principles of the self-organizing system
  —value for openness

2) Conditions in the field of the *musical space*:

  —belief in the *power* of sound to change and form
  —commitment
  —a value for relating
  —containment

3) Conditions in the *field of play*:

—belief that through playing in sound, creative development will occur
—a value for play and modeling
—openness

4) Conditions in the field of *ritual*:

—constants
—repetition
—containment

5) Conditions in the *particular state of consciousness*:

—fluidity
—the state itself (between the abstract and the concrete)
—openness

6) Conditions in the *field of power*:

—building up of energy to a threshold point
—actualization and action
—containment

7) Conditions in the field of the *creative process*:

—the process, including all previous conditions

It is important to remember that all newly

forming fields have their own conditions and also
retain or discard previous conditions, depending on
the requirements of the new field. That is to say, the
sorting out, retaining and discarding of conditions
comes out of the logic of the self-organizing system,
and the necessary organizational aspects for each
new field coming into being.

Hearing the Play

And how do we see this logic of the self-
organizing system, or more importantly, how do we
hear it?

First, it is important to state that the principle
of self-organizing is an assumption inherent in the
model—the drive in living matter to perfect itself.

It is implied in the Navaho inspired-phrase "a
movement toward beauty is a movement toward
wholeness."

We assume that given the proper conditions, a
client and therapist will:

1) move toward beauty
    or
2) drive to perfect him/herself
    or
3) self-organize in the best way possible, given
    the conditions in any field, in a given
    moment in time.

Perhaps the easiest way to observe this process and
hear it is in the context of the musical improvisation.
And the *Field of Play*, though a general model, was

designed from the context of spontaneous music-making.

It was also designed out of one-to-one work. The model can serve practitioners in a variety of situations through a variety of techniques. This is because the world of our work, is essentially, *musical*, man in relationship to music. Even if we are using verbal techniques, even if we are giving music lessons, or leading a rhythm band, or a handbell choir, the music of our experience is essential. We can hear this music. In a sense this is the vision and hope of the holographic paradigm, the implied form, under the surface of our experience, which reflects the whole of our experience, no matter what our explicate reality may be.

The simplicity and clarity of the one-to-one work helps us to focus on a relationship with only two individuals. This gives us a good foundation to then brainstorm about contexts which contain more than two participants.

Spontaneous or improvisational music provides a context in which to experiment and play with sound and thus allow the participants to design an expressive form which reflects and actualizes their natural tendency toward self-organization.

The musical improvisation provides a supportive environment in which they can experiment until they find authentic expressions which do in fact reflect and actualize deep growth and change. They receive the benefit of expression and communication in the immediacy of the sound, which serves as an image and a change agent.

In this sense, the musical improvisation is both

subjective and objective—subjective in that it reflects the inner life—human feeling, thought and experience, and objective in that it creates an external object, i.e., the music.

Thus one can "hear" the reflection of one's own being—appreciating, adapting, adjusting and experimenting and potentially moving toward the highest level of organization which one is capable of in that particular moment in time.

This is the relationship and the interplay between man and music and in essence the nature of music therapy.

Chapter five

The Interplay of the Fields

Theoretical Description
Description of a Music Therapy Session

It has become a sort of principle of modern thought that the two attributes of totality and reflective consciousness cannot be associated with the same subject... Totality can only be grasped at the point where it gathers. And such a point is perfectly conceivable since, in the realm of spirit-matter, nothing limits the inner complexity of a point.
(From Pierre Teillard de Chardin, *Human Energy*)

Theoretical Description

The first important step in the *Field of Play* is the acknowledgement of an *aesthetic*. An *aesthetic* is a field or environment containing conditions for the creation of beauty. In the music therapy experience, the human person is an aesthetic and thus an environment of being and acting through relationship and music, with a particular attention for human growth and development. As an aesthetic, the human person holds love as an informing energy which provides conditions in the field.

The process in the field of the *aesthetic* has to do with changing places acknowledged and developed through musical experience. The field of the aesthetic is a place which appreciates what is present, yet has an anticipation for and belief in what is possible in the emerging moment, all this in reference to learning, growth and change. It has to do with stretching the boundaries of what we consider our limitations—for client and therapist.

The aesthetic forms a defined, yet open space: one which provides safety and support, one which receives all being and acting as part of the ongoing process of change (defined through the emerging relationship between client and therapist).

Anticipation is another important condition in this field. The therapist is committed to maintaining a posture which waits enduringly for the slightest micromovement, sound or pattern indicative of *a movement toward wholeness*. This movement could be dramatic or subtle. These movements are initiated by the client although they may be inspired by the therapist. Movements toward wholeness reflect the logic of the self-orgnanizing system. The therapist notices, receives and responds to this movement, signified by patterns and textures of sound. If the patient is willing to share, that is, not only express, but also communicate this changing process, a step has been taken toward communication, relationship and rehabilitation.

Fundamentally, the therapist is limited in terms of what s/he is able or willing to notice. But it is hoped that through her/his own human experience and skill, s/he will notice and respond to some significant aspect of the patient's stretching boundaries in the direction of positive change.

The field also resonates in many domains and dimensions. For example, even though it is moving toward emotions in its primary intention it has effects in the cognitive and sensorimotor areas as well. All expressions are received, acknowledged and valued.

Each *aesthetic* is highly individualized and never value-free. Values or beliefs, even though they may be nonverbal, constitute conditions in the field. In the *aesthetic* of the therapist the following values and thus conditions are present. They form a foundation for all seven fields.

1) Value for a particular form of beauty, which has to do with changing places particularly in human growth, development and learning, feelings of expansion, feelings

of appreciation for all the variables in the field (including attitudes, beliefs, behaviors, observers, light, extra sound, etc.) inclusively, openness;

2) Value for an existential approach which views each moment as the only moment in time in the given field;

3) Belief in the principles of the self-organizing system—that each human being is unique and that part of each human, no matter how deeply traumatized, holds the most logical and effective plan for the whole of his/her development, as well as each step in the sequence of development and change.

In the final analysis, the *aesthetic* represents a way of being which carries information and conditions. It stresses the importance of subtle, non-verbal cues communicated before the onset of concrete activity. It represents the sum total of who we are, and transmits information about who we are on a subtle level before the onset of relationship. Being "who we are" communicates a field of being and establishes conditions to which clients respond during improvisation. The conditions of the *aesthetic* also grant support and permission for particular parts of the client to emerge and evolve within the *musical space* and the *field of play*.

When the *aesthetics* of client and therapist

overlap, that which is able to come forth and create a relational field emerges. Once again, the logic of a natural self-organization is in play. A commitment is made to this new field when there is a point of engagement in the musical gestures. This new field is called the *musical space*. It is a space which is closed, i.e., a private space which is reserved only for therapist and client. The musical improvisation is the meeting place between the abstract and the concrete. It represents abstract phenomena such as ideas, emotions, attitudes, etc., yet is a sensorial phenomenon in sound forms.

In the *musical space*, the client and therapist merge into a pool of human expression and communication. They become equally significant participants and formers of the being and acting in this new field through relationship of the two. The participants create this space through their relationship to each other represented in the music. The playing of music is a developmental action and represents whatever each selects to place into the field of the *musical space*, once again demonstrating organization. The commitment to play music together is the most consistent and reliable condition in this field.

The environment which was first formed by the *aesthetic* is now realized through the *musical space*. The music, as created by client and therapist together form the space just as the *aesthetic* previously formed the space prior to the engaging activity between therapist and client. Therapist and client come together in the creative act of making music.

The *musical space* is a self-contained safety zone which develops out of the relationship between the two participants. This relationship, which becomes contained in a mutually created space now becomes the most formative condition in the field.

Once the trust has been established in the *musical space* and the participants have developed a relationship through sound which creates a home base or constant, it is then possible for the *musical space* to expand into the *field of play*.

The *field of play* is a new field, one which includes the *aesthetics* and the *musical space*. It grows out of these two, yet expands into a field of experimentation, play and modeling. It is an open space, which is more conducive to innovation and more fluid in nature.

Each participant *plays* and *models* forms which hold meaning for the individual creating the sound. The client improvises and searches for meaningful patterns and sounds. The therapist follows the patterns and forms of the client to intensify the texture—to explore and develop the feelings or thoughts within the improvisational form. Similarly, the therapist presents models of meaningful sounds which s/he determines may be useful to the client from her experience. When a patten or form is intuitively embraced by client, therapist or both, the assumption is that this form holds meaning for the client and/or therapist and therefore will be played or developed for a while—to investigate, meaning, communication, expression, growth.

Through this relationship of play and modelling

within the musical improvisation, each selects the pieces or parts or wholes of musical patterning which make sense in the authentic expression of the self and in the mutually creative process. Again, this is a form of organizing sound.

Hopefully, the openness of the aesthetics and the trust developed in the *musical space* continues to function in the *field of play* as therapist and client engage in spontaneous playing with patterns, rhythms and sounds, harmonies and melodies, consonance and dissonance, dynamics, etc. The assumption is that *authentic sounds* will emerge and provide the starting point for development. Most often these authentic expressions have to do with deep emotions, which, for whatever reason, are inexpressible in verbal language. The expression and communication of these emotions initiates growth and change.

It is believed that within the process of the musical improvisation development will occur. The process is the product.

The *field of play* contains four interactive elements or fields: *ritual, a particular state of consciousness, power, creative process*. These fields overlap to also create conditions and relationships which develop the potential of the *field of play* over time.

Ritual is the set of repeatable forms created through the conditions present at the time of the session. These forms can include the overall form of the session itself and all of the various musical forms expressed in the musical improvisation, and any other pattern which is repeated in the ritual space. The actual playing of music is a constant. The circumstances are reliable, replicable and constant—the room, entering the room and greetings, the action of verbal and musical dialogue, moments of silence and stopping, playing again through several progressions, endings, goodbyes.

Hopefully, the ritual forms, which emerge organically from the experience, particularly in the musical improvisation itself, will provide another ground base, just as the *musical space*. This field of support allows the participants to try out innovation within the security of constants, or within the framework of the repeatable forms which have emerged in the *field of play* thus far.

The most important condition in this field, then, is the condition of constants. Once again, this emerging structure demonstrates a tendency to organize through identifying these constants in the field. Once again ritual interplays with the *aesthetic*, the *musical space* and the *field of play*, representing an organic process.

A *particular state of consciousness* is a field of focused relaxation and intense concentration, yet playfulness. Once again, it is a state between the abstract and the concrete and thus bridges two realities. One is aware of feelings and thoughts yet also engaged in the sensorial realm of creation of sound forms. This creation assumes an ability to select and screen input aesthetically as it is presented through the results of musical improvisation. Some sound patterns and forms are accepted, some are rejected, depending on their success or failure as authentic expressions. In this state of consciousness one is self-motivated. It is a motivational state which plays itself into change through musical form. It thus reflects another type of organization and also includes all previous fields and conditions. It is an open field which allows one to travel in the dimension of consciousness into a fluid reality which is not contingent on circumstance, e.g., disability. The most outstanding condition in this field is the state itself.

Power is a phenomenon which sets the patient in motion. It represents the field which is created through a relationship between will and receptivity which yields inner motivation and action. It is critical to human growth and development and essential for change. If the patient has been favorably inclined toward the previous elements, the *particular state of conciousness* has prepared him or her for the inner motivation, the *ritual* would have given him or her the ground base needed for experimentation, and s/he has gathered and continues to gather substance through the ongoing *musical space* and the *field of play*. Therefore it is possible to allow interaction between the state of inner motivation and receptivity in order to actualize power.

Power is a contained phenomenon and is associated also with the accumulation of enough energy to initiate change. Therefore it is a threshhold point. It builds over time until there is a natural breakthrough. In the musical form, it is most easily recognized through initiation of expression and assertiveness on the part of the client. The most important condition in this field is actualization so that the client can experience the concrete results of his musical gestures, hear his/her own power in this movement and thus maintain an ongoing feeding of the state of inner motivation and receptivity to new forms.

Creative process is the last field in the model. It is a result of the interplay among all the previous elements yet it is the process itself, as well as the product. The process is field-creating but also self-creating or self-actualizing. It is organic in that it emerges sequentially from each previous influence and existential in that it proceeds from and to each moment in time. This is demonstrated in patterns of sound or receptivity to sound in the experience. This is the holographic nature of the model.

Description of Music Therapy Session

Even before the onset of therapy it is very important to attend to comfort of the settng. Both the room and the therapist must indicate a safe and inviting environment for the client. Some factors to be considered are lighting, temperature, acoustics, privacy. There must be easy access to the piano.

The therapist should be pleasantly dressed and be in a calm, confident and receptive state. It is important to say a kind of prayer—to call forth the necessary skills and talents available in the vast range of possibilities within the aesthetic of the therapist. It is hoped that the resources which are most appropriate and which will be most life-enhancing for the client will function to the maximum degree. In this spirit, it is also important that the therapist clarify her/his intentions for the situation.

In the session with Jack I attended to these considerations as much as possible. My intention for him was that he would feel safe enough to allow the best steps in his human development to emerge within the session and that he would retain this growth with enough insight and intuition to transfer it into other areas of his rehabilitation process. My secondary intention was that I would be able, clearly and confidently, to meet him in the music in order to best facilitate this process as a guide and resource person.

This was Jack's first music therapy session. Initially he displayed an obvious level of anxiety. Since it was the first session, I was also a bit nervous. The presence of video cameras and equipment also probably created tension in the room. The presence of the hospital staff psychologist was reassuring to Jack, since he was a familiar, supportive person.

When Jack entered the room, I asked him where he would like to sit. I gave him the choice of which side of the piano to play from.

"Where would you feel the most comfortable," I asked.

Jack took his place at the bass end.
Jack replied: "I very rarely play."

To me this indicated an initial fear of expectations. What would be required of him in this situation?

I attempted to create an atmosphere of maximum flexibility to let Jack know that there were no rules per se and that the expectation level to perform was very low. I reiterated the invitation to sit whereever he liked and proceeded to explain the soft structure which would create a container for the experience.

I introduced myself and said: "What has Cliff (the psychologist) said to you about this?"

Jack replied: "Very little. He said I was going to play the piano. I don't really play, but I said alright."

"This is literally 'play'", I said, "fooling around at the piano...not to play by written music, or any set thing. Basically, just having fun. I'll just follow you—complement, play along, or imitate."

Jack laughed at this.

"If you like a sound your hand just happens to land on," I said, "you just fool around with it. If you don't like it, move on to some other sound combination. Mainly enjoy yourself. Go for as long as you want. Stop when you want."

Jack continued to laugh intermittently through this first bit of conversation to relieve his tension. I joined him in the humor, smiling and letting him know that his laughter was totally acceptable to me.

Then he said: "I don't know where to begin."

I said: "Sometimes you can start just like this."

At this point I randomly smashed down five consecutive notes simultaneously. This represented the first piano sound.

Up to this point I would say that *we were getting to know each other's aesthetic* through conversation, tone of voice, body language, gesture and intuition. This was a form of personal play, finding a place to relate through our personalities. *The initiation of sound on the musical instrument was my indication that I was ready to engage in the second stage, the musical space.*

Jack then quite quickly began to play the piano *indicating his intention to join the musical space.* He played very standard, sequences of broken triads, beginning with C, E, G and progressing to D, E, F with the same 1-3-5 sequences up the keyboard in my direction.

I imitated his sounds and forms in two octaves in the treble range. Then on his fifth triad, I offered a simple modification, 1-5-3 sequence in triad instead of 1-3-5. I also played the two octaves in harmony with each other once, maintaining the form of the third. Jack acknowledged the subtle change of mood created by these changes by a little chuckle, not of the nervous kind. We "took turns" in our playing.

I continued to follow his lead, yet modify here and there slightly.

> Then I said: "It doesn't have to sound nice. Just if you want it to."
>
> Jack said: "I kind of do. I hope it does."
>
> I reassured him by saying: "It sounds very nice."

I hoped that this would give him permission to go on. But most importantly, it indicated to him that his goals were my goals and I thought he was accomplishing his goals, e.g., to "sound nice."

At this point Jack became more experimental and broke away from the one previous octave range he had used. This indicated to me that he initiated the third stage, the *field of play*. The feeling was one of bursting forth, going further afield. In the musical form this was indicated by moving beyond the fixed tonality, the 1-3-5 broken triadic structure, extending across four octaves, thus taking up more space on the piano. His dynamics also increased in volume. He made bigger sounds, more sounds. He was no longer tentative. Although he chose to keep returning to the chordal emphasis, he would also experiment with other possibilities—one note, unusual combinations of notes beyond the safe 1-3-5 pattern, etc.

Jack began to concentrate intensely, listening and judging the sounds. I continued to play with the idea of supporting his experimentation. When I felt that he was tensing up in a non-productive way, I played some staccato sounds to break up the tension.

> Then I said: "Remember that there are no mistakes."

He played a soft sound and I said: "Nice. That's romantic."

This was to reinforce his desire to have his sound be "nice" and to indicate that I was picking up a specific quality from his music. I wanted him to know that I was being informed about his aesthetic through his sound creation and that I accepted and appreciated it as well as interpreted it in my own way. It seemed to me that Jack barely heard this comment because of his deep concentration.

Then Jack wanted variety. He kept extending his range of sounds and experimenting with different tonal structures.

However, I noticed that in his experimenting he had a tendency to return to G minor tonality. At one point when he was meandering through the options in this tonality, he spontaneously said "Hmm, nice." This was the one spontaneous explicit indication that he had been pleased with his creative efforts. I had already noticed the G Minor tendency and his comment reinforced its significance to Jack. To me that meant that at least, for the time being, Jack considered this "territory" to be home base. He had established his own supportive field in a tonal range.

I took this as a clear cue. My new improvisational strategy was that I stayed primarily in the G Minor range to provide the new supportive context which had emerged from the *field of play*. In a sense I assumed a portion of Jack's identity at this point. Hopefully, my playing created a supportive context which found its source in his own choices. Thus my support mirrored Jack supporting himself. *He could thus engage in the field of play in a new way.*

The establishment of the tonality in G Minor created a "home base". Hopefully, the security of having a home base in the sound would encourage Jack to have more freedom of exploration.

This improvisational section in the middle of the session, based in G Minor, represents the core of the therapy. Jack was in a particular state of deep concentration, yet relaxation (*a particular state of consciousness*). He accepted the constant of the G Minor tonality and the chordal structures (*ritual*). His improvisation was strongest in this segment (*power*). Jack's improvisation was highly creative in this sequence, a great variety of sounds, combinations of sounds with varying texture and dynamics (*creative process*).

This was the peak.

After a time, Jack ended the sequence. He broke away from the tonality and began to look for something else. In one of these experimentations, he said:

"I've done those before. Let's see. . ." (searching for new sounds). He also said: "What else can I do here."

These comments indicated to me the seeking of even more variety. He had "played out" the themes in the G Minor tonality. My assumption was that these sounds and moods were Jack's implicate forms, patterns and self-organizing order. I also assumed that the sounds implied meanings and were significant to Jack. At the time we did not verbalize the meanings, and in fact, the meanings may have gone beyond the reach of words. However, he found them and used them. Then he played a chromatic progression down to bass. I copied and followed his movement down the piano.

For awhile Jack returned intermittently to the G Minor tones with a different texture than before—more bold. But he continued to move gradually away from these sounds for more variety.

Then Jack played some sounds he didn't like.

He was getting tired and sighed. Jack stopped playing and asked:

"What next?"

I suggested that we switch sides of the piano. Jack went to the bass. I took the treble. Jack played solid F Major tones.

Then he played another sound he didn't like and said: "That was a sour sounding note from me."

He said: "I'm getting worn out."

Then he took the back of his hand and ran it down the entire keyboard. I did the same.

We both laughed at an apparently good ending.

I told him that if he was ready to end, then that was the end.

I asked Jack if he enjoyed the session. He replied in the affirmative.

Then he asked Cliff if that was enough, and laughed.

Jack left.

Chapter six

Practice

Clinical Work
Clinical Work with Individuals
Clinical Work with Groups
Research
Training
The Field of Music Therapy

The healer had to be ruthless to create the proper setting for the spirit's intervention. (From Carlos Castaneda, *The Power of Silence*)

Clinical Work

Clinical Work with Individuals

The model of the *field of play* is based on the simplest and most basic form of clinical practice, that is, the one-to-one dialogue between therapist and client in the music therapy experience.

"Simple" here refers only to numbers of people. Even though numerically we might think of this dialogue as simple, geometrically, it is highly complex. (See figure 8 on page 119.)

Removing the color from the model demonstrates the complexity. It is difficult to describe the music therapy experience on a flat one-dimensional surface. If we assume that this is an expanding, holographic systems model, it will expand in every direction, creating more conditions, relationships, fields and organizations, upon conditions, relationships, fields and organizations exponentially. The *Field of Play* is a "field matrix" which centers and holds a process.

It is an energy system.

The *Field of Play* invites the clinician into a heartfelt examination of the "conditions" which he or she brings into the music therapy experience. Conditions may be considered to be anything which determines the characteristics and features of the space which is the *aesthetic*. There are hundreds of non-verbal cues exuded by the music therapist in the realm of subtle sense. The interior life is reflected in the external. The interior life may include beliefs, attitudes, memories of life experiences, etc. These are reflected in the more obvious conditions such as

Diagram 8: The Field of Play

the behaviour and style of the therapist. All are contained in "the field". Clients not only see and hear these conditions in the obvious expressions of our personality and our use of tools such as musical instruments, but they also sense them through more subtle expressions, such as tone of voice, body language, posture, rhythm of speech, energy level, choice of technique, etc.

In addition these conditions are constantly reorganizing themselves with new input. Our form of beauty is dynamic.

Every condition has an aspect of strength and an aspect of limitation. It is our ability to embrace creative paradox and ambiguity which allows us the possibility to manage our conditions. The way we recognize and tend to a condition will determine its effect in the field.

The next consideration of the clinician involves an equally heartfelt examination of the conditions of the client. In this case, it is particularly important to recognize conditions which are subtle and non-verbal. When we work with people who have special needs our tendency is to focus only on acute conditions or chronic conditions or symptoms or disablements. This limits our sense of wholeness and beauty.

Very often the quiet, more subtle conditions which we choose to ignore, are the ones which will assist our clients the most in the music therapy experience. If we as clinicians, respond to these conditions, the ones which are perhaps only implied, we encourage their stability in the *musical space*, and thus healing can begin.

The next question for the clinician is: *How can I do my part in the design and establishment of the musical space?* This is a consideration which will require a great deal of discrimination on the part of the music therapist for s/he is essentially the guardian of the space.

Practical considerations of level of distraction, comfort of style, selection of rhythmic and melodic patterns, staff observation and participation are critical. The containment of the environment is a necessary step in the creation of the *musical space.* This containment allows for the development of trust and subsequently the movement into the *field of play.*

The therapist gives attention to changing conditions in each field as it emerges throughout the course of a music therapy session on a subtle or obvious level.

This *field of play* contains four interacting fields—*ritual, a particular state of consciousness, power* and *creative process.* This is the process in which the style and individuality of the clinician exert the most authority and creativity. The *aesthetic,* the *musical space* and the *field of play* serve as primary fields, and stages. *Ritual, a particular state of consciousness, power* and *creative process* serve as secondary fields and offer the therapist a chance to play with his or her own sequencing preference.

A clinician may use more or less of these secondary fields. The order may vary, depending on each person's style. What one clinician defines as *ritual* may be totally unrecognizable as *ritual* to another. In case of induction in "guided imagery through music," the *particular state of consciousness* may play a more dominant and obvious role than in the use of behaviorist methods. Some improvisational music techniques which focus on uncovering creative resources, may seem to place more value on *creative process* than structured music lessons. *Power* may seem more obvious in a stage when a client "sings" a song or performs a "skat" than in a more subtle stage of power when the person is not singing, yet the heart is pounding and still stuck in the throat.

The important perception for the clinician is the *underlying dynamic structure of the experience seen through sound and silence* as it is moving through space and time and his/her relationship to that moving structure, the *Field of Play*.

Is it time for opening or closing?

Is a threshhold building to power?

Whatever technique I use, can I sense a *creative process*?

Are there enough repeatable forms to assist the development of a safe space for innovation—a ground from which to fly?

Is there a state of focused, yet relaxed concentration—a vibrant, clear space which is waiting for sound, for creation?

What are the patterns emerging from each field which facilitate organization?

These are some of the questions for the clinician working in a one-to-one setting in music therapy.

Clinical Work with Groups

When the clinician encounters a group, the

complexity intensifies. Yet the simplicity of the basic human one-to-one dialogue remains a constant.

The group becomes an *aesthetic* in and of itself. It takes on a life of its own, a dynamic of its own. So each group member has a relationship to the *aesthetic* of the group.

All of the considerations which apply to an individual person as *aesthetic* apply to group as *aesthetic*. What are the conditions of the field of "group"? A *musical space* is also established between each group member and group, as well as a *field of play* with its secondary fields of *ritual, a particular state of consciousness, power*, and *creative process*.

In the *Field of Play*, whenever two aesthetics link, a sevenfold interactive process begins.

On a subtle level every person in a group is interacting with every other person, even if this does not appear to be the case. In addition, just as each group member has a relationship to the *aesthetic* of "group", each group member also has a discrete relationship with the clinician.

Altogether, this makes group work in music therapy highly complex. Sometimes the powerful tendency of music toward socialization, integration and organization, has us leaving the resources of the subtle domain far too quickly. We forget to listen to the sounds before the sound, the silent pulse.

The group music therapy clinician observes timing for opening and closing. In a closed structure, over time, patterns become well-defined, which is part of their great value. However in order for there to be a creative process, those closed structures must eventually open, thus the on-going dynamic between opening and closing continues.

In some forms of music therapy such as spontaneous musicmaking, it is equally important for the clinician to observe the timing of when to close the field or to hear the client closing the field. For example, a period of cacaphony may extend so far as to fall into a terrifying chaos, instead of one which is exploring potential. Some cacaphony may serve as a healthy catharsis, then the reorganizing can occur. It is the responsibility of the clinician to know how to design the space for a healthy movement toward wholeness.

This is only the tip of the iceberg into clinical considerations.

Clinical work might be imagined as the heartbeat of our profession. We want the human person to be able to function in his or her best quality of life. And the way we do this is through music.

On a bad day, when we have a difficult session, we may come home and say "Why am I doing this?" Meaning seems vague, our sense of purpose challenged.

On a day when we have had a particularly moving music therapy session with an autistic child who played only one note on the glockenspiel, but this being the first note ever, we may come home and be overwhelmed with joy.

The *Field of Play* says: This is a process. The highs and lows are expressed in the music therapy experience in an ebb and flow, an inward and outward movement, just like the overall rhythm of life on Earth, just like the tides, like the seasons, like birth and death. It goes on.

The *Field of Play* attempts to support both the clinical and more global needs of the music therapy practitioner. The theoretical model can be applied to any population, used with any technique. It is a general model, a soft architecture to support the work.

Research

Music therapy research is an area which is greatly in need of expansion. Chapter three highlights many issues in the philosophy and theory of science which refer to music therapy. Most of these issues center around a search for harmony between logic and intuition, an attention to process, an appreciation for the aesthetic dimension, sensation, consciousness, and most important, the essential elements of our experience as music therapists.

The *Field of Play* invites researchers in music therapy to investigate research methods such as phenomenology, which are descriptive in nature. Music therapy constitutes an interplay between subjective and objective realities. Often descriptive methods are not considered because of our fear of subjectivity. Yet the element of subjectivity is present in every research design. The researcher is part of the process. His or her values and attitudes are present in the selection of research populations and methods. Assumptions which move and motivate a researcher bear a direct influence on design of studies. In a sense, subjectivity communicates our humanness because the expressions which immanate from the subjective constitute our response to being human and inform our decisions about the tools we use for work. The conditions of the researcher are part of the work and always have an influence on the results of the study.

Many research methods which are used in music therapy are borrowed from other disciplines. The *Field of Play* offers a challenge to people interested in music therapy research. Can we begin to design our own research tools, which are informed by our direct experience in music therapy?

In order to do this we need to gather more description so that we can dialogue, compare, contrast and search for underlying patterns in our experience.

In my study of Native American systems I have come to understand the great value of a "story". Stories describe life. They gather a tradition. They lay a groundwork and reflect the implied patterns of experience. They inspire the imagination. They communicate "immediacy", the rhythm, tone and texture of our life on Earth. In the ancient traditions, the term story and "song" were interchangeable. Song carries spirit.

Often spirit is communicated through "process". Ideally, descriptive studies are not invested in outcome. They have a pace and timing which allows a processorial structure to reveal itself over time. Proof is not the point. We need lots of description in all the different media of communication—the written word, audiotapes, videotapes, photographs, conceptual designs, etc.

We must build a body of literature which explores the many aspects of description from theory to practice, in every population, in every technique, in every country. Then we can have Kuhn's dialogue in a community of professionals about a shared phenomenon.

I have attempted to establish a dialogue about

a shared phenomenon in my own research. In my dissertation I was interested in the possibility of designing new language. I've been testing out this language with many music therapists, particularly members of the Phoenecia Music Therapy Retreat Community. The type of question which is asked over and over again in these encounters is: How would *you* describe this musical improvisation? How would you describe the interaction between therapist and client? Can you describe the presence of the principles of music in verbal techniques used by music therapist? Can you see and describe a process?

In a more formal aspect of the study, I also gathered a panel of professionals related to music therapy, but not necessarily in the field. I wanted to know if this new language would be comprehensible to others. My panel included:

1) a dance/movement therapist
2) a psychiatrist
3) a neuropsychologist
4) an existential phenomenologist
5) a musicologist
6) a composer
7) an acupuncturist and practitionner of Eastern medicine.

Each panel member received:

1) a videotape of clinical improvisation, which I felt demonstrated the seven fields in the sound;
2) a list of brief definitions of the seven fields;
3) a brief description of the client;
4) a brief description of the hospital;
5) a transcription of the verbal interaction during

the session as a guide to the videotape;
6) a 21-item questionnaire.

Through the questionnaire, each panel member was invited to participate in the phenomenological inquiry by wearing their own set of glasses to view the music therapy experience on the videotape. They were asked if they could see or hear or sense or perceive in any way an *aesthetic*, a *musical space*, a *field of play*, *ritual*, a *particular state of consciousness*, *power* or *creative process* as described in my definitions. They were also asked how each of their definitions would differ from mine. As well, there were questions which encouraged open-ended feedback.

This system served to refine and check the definitions of the fields and to create a discussion forum for the new language. The research design created a dialogue. The holographic color model was designed when a panel member asked me to draw a "topography" of the process.

This is an example of how research designs can make good use of descriptive methods.

Training

A good first step in the training of music therapists is a commitment to theory—from the onset of training. There are certain questions which we can ask our students in order to lay the groundwork for a healthy developmental process of theory creation. For example:

1) What are your underlying assumptions about healing and therapy?

2)   What is your general world view?
3)   What are your beliefs?

Even if trainees do not have answers to these questions, they begin a process of inquiry, which hopefully will initiate an awareness of the value of theory. These questions encourage a recognition of thought patterns which will eventually lead them into designing a creative theoretical basis for their work. This is the appreciation of one's subtle music.

Trainees need, as well, to develop a whole person approach to function within the *Field of Play*. They need skills to manage the great paradox of a constant flux between open and closed systems. They need to develop both logical and intuitive skills.

The best way to learn about the process of change is through personal experience. Yet it is difficult to build this into a university training program or require it as an admissions criterion. A person who has had to develop the strength and resources required in a transformative life experience will have at least an implied understanding of the *Field of Play*.

In general, the question of training challenges our systems as they are currently designed. This is an area which needs a great deal of attention from the music therapy community.

The Field of Music Therapy

The field of music therapy practices in the culture-at-large. As a body it interplays with many other fields, the most obvious of which provide human service and generally are concerned with the human condition. As a field we bring a unique set of conditions to interplay with society and culture.

This position carries a responsibility for deep examination of the influence we may have on the culture-at-large. For almost a half century the clinical practice of music therapy has been growing and changing, developing a body or research, building a professional identity. If we extend this professional identity to include the more ancient uses of music for healing, our tradition extends back historically to some of the first human gestures on Earth.

If we apply even the smallest amount of future vision, we see increasing documentation in the sciences of psychoimmunology, neurophysiology, biology, physics, and general consciousness studies to support the inclusion of music therapy in delivery of any human service which encourages change—everything from cancer to learning disabilities to the development of creativity in psychotherapy. The power of sound and image to facilitate change is being documented at an increasing rate.

It is time for us to focus on the uniqueness of music therapy experience so that we can bring this richness and depth into the culture-at-large. When someone asks a music therapy clinician to describe his or her experience in a language which does not come as close as possible to describing our most *direct experience*, it is time to say "no." It is time to say "No, that word or phrase or term does not match. But come and observe my work and we'll brainstorm about how to describe what's going on."

We have worked for the time to develop descriptions of our inner life—the life of music therapy. The time is now.

Chapter seven

The Field and Beyond

"We are men and our lot is to learn and to be hurled into inconceivable new worlds."

"Are there any new worlds for us really?" I asked half in jest.

"We have exhausted nothing, you fool," he said imperatively. "*Seeing* is for impeccable men. Temper your spirit now, become a warrior, learn to *see*, and you'll know that there is no end to the new worlds for our vision."

(From Carlos Castaneda, *A Separate Reality*)

The search for the *Field of Play* has been quite a humbling experience, yet an exciting and expanding one. The one thing which I have learned overall from this experience is a validation of the complexity of human communication. There seem to be an infinite number of variables which combine and organize to create the "*aesthetic* which is the human person." I now feel the beauty of communication in a different way. Specifically, that when it truly does happen, it is indeed a miracle.

We each view the world through a different set of glasses, fashioned uniquely by "who we are". With the great diversity of these views, human objectivity and general theory-building seem insurmountable tasks. I like Joseph Campbell's concept of "human constants", and Kuhn's idea of a dialoguing community of professionals. Through identifying the constants in our experience and perceptions, perhaps there is some hope of establishing a home base in which to dialogue in a community of humans, who are indeed fragile and vulnerable creatures, given the inadequacies of our communication systems.

Because of our great vulnerability and fear, we have also, as a culture, avoided a commitment to the creative process, a place full of nutrients for human growth and development, yet often too vast and uncontrollable for our minds to comprehend. The *Field of Play* is about the creative process. It proposes one way for us to approach the process of human growth, which allows us our necessary security, and thus the freedom to "play" with creative alternatives.

A commitment to the creative process may be one way of curing what Argüelles has described as "holonomic amnesia." We might find our way back into an intuitive awareness which guides and informs our communication. In order to follow this rather terrifying journey, humans need love.

The *Field of Play* focuses on non-verbal communication as a means to this intuitive source, a guide which can help us to discover "implicit patterns," subtleties contained deep within the human psyche, which perhaps defy our logical orientation, yet are moving us toward wholeness more wholely.

In chaper one, the question is put forth:

Is it possible to formulate a language to describe the music therapy experience and create one of many possible general models which accurately reflect music therapy process, yet which can be understood and used by professionals in other fields?

The *Field of Play* is exploratory in nature. It considers the primordial aspect of our experience, the largely undefined field of experience. The only use for a new language is that it somehow assists us in understanding a process which is not easily described by language which is idiosyncratic to the culture and time. The language developed here ring's of Merleau-Ponty's "wild meaning." It seeks to contact Argüelles' "aboriginal continuity," our more primitive knowing which keeps us in touch with process, with Earth, with sense.

The birthing of new language which recovers this sense in a contemporary world may be difficult.

However, the research question ultimately will only fully be answered in the application of the language and the model to praxis—to clinical music therapy practice and research, to teaching and training music therapists and other health professionals.

In chapter two a review of the tradition of theory in music therapy reveals tendencies to describe the music therapy experience through conditions, fields, relationships and organization. These tendencies resonated with my own approach. My particular pair of phenomenological glasses may have colored my perception, and guided me into seeking support for my own theoretical model. The review identifies a starting place in its search for "theoretical roots."

In chapter three a rationale is designed for the use of phenomenological research in music therapy. Phenomenological research, particularly when it is designed along existential, hermeneutic and heuristic lines offers a place for the eye of the artist, a connection to sense phenomena, and a structure for the creative process. In addition, it is demonstrated that systems thinking paves a healthy path for the Earth connection, sensation, model-making. Both allow an entry for the development of consciousness. I would conclude that this particular research style is highly appropriate for music therapy.

Chapter four describes the theoretical framework. This framework embraces the four elements identified in chapter two and uses them as criteria for the seven fields of the *aesthetic*, the *music space*, the *field of play*, *ritual*, a *particular state of consciousness*, *power* and *creative process*. All seven elements hold the foundation of the theoretical field. This foundation is defined in chapter two and carried through to chapter four, primarily in the work of William Sears, Helen Bonny and my own previous work. Thus I believe that the model The *Field of Play* is in harmony with the roots of theory in music therapy. A visual holographic model offers a conceptual design of the spatial interplay of the theory.

Chapter five offers both abstract and concrete examples of how the *Field of Play* can describe the process of music therapy.

Chapter six provides some basic guidelines for the music therapy clinician for both one-to-one and group sessions. It also addresses important issues about research. Training is briefly discussed. The place of the field of music therapy in the culture-at-large completes this section.

In an article entitled "Field Consciousness and Field Ethics", in the book *The Holographic Paradigm and Other Paradoxes* (Wilber), Renee Weber describes the operating principle of David Bohm's "implicate order." Weber states that Bohm's basic contention is that "love is an informing energy."

I have always believed that if we can somehow manage to keep in touch with our "love of work", we will also manage to gather the appropriate pieces of information which center around, expand and develop that work. In order to stay in contact with this loving, informing energy, I have focused on whole memories of the direct experience of music therapy. If ever I became lost in a maze of data and ideas, I returned to these memories as a clear and powerful lifeline to the heart and soul of the work. In this lifeline, which travels across twenty years, particular clients, particular pieces of literature, particular observations of colleagues, particular dialogues with colleagues emerge as information. But there is another level of "information" which I experience as "subtle sense". It is non-verbal. It is a sensation which travels far beyond words. It is music. I can only hope that this text communicates this memory, this lifeline, this subtle sense.

We work with concepts and language as a means to understand the processes of human development. But concepts and language only describe. They cannot *be* our experience. They can only convey our experience in a limited fashion. Concepts mediate the abstract and the concrete, spirit and matter.

The *Field of Play* is an ecological or environmental model. It is an organic, process-oriented energy system. It is based on a definition of beauty and wholeness which conforms closely to ancient healing concepts.

This is another tip of another iceberg which needs a lot of attention. I am firmly convinced that we need to come to terms with the conceptual level of ancient healing systems which systematically employed the arts for healing. Through this study, perhaps, we can recover some our own lost sense.

An unfortunate situation in the contemporary world is the commercialization of the "techniques" of these ancient healing systems. This, I feel, is a great tragedy, not only for the Native American peoples who are once again commercialized in the name of progress, but also for the contemporary culture who receives only the most fleeting and colorful benefit of ancient ritual forms. If we take on a serious study of the underlying concepts of these rituals, try to comprehend their meaning in context, we may be able to design appropriate techniques for modern day life which recover our value for a sense of our connectedness to "environment", the Earth and the human person. Likewise, it would be equally tragic for music therapy to develop as yet another profane technology. Where is the soul of the work?

Eagle's model of the interdisciplinary nature of the art pertains to our dialogue beyond the field, our relationship with other fields. We need to seek, describe, define, the center of music therapy, the uniqueness, in order to come to the external dialogue with clear articulations.

Through our study of ancient healing systems we come to the worlds of anthropology and ethnomusicology. We also come to the fields of philosophy and religious studies.

All of these disciplines address the non-verbal, the importance of communication systems of the arts, the development of psyche and intuition, the development of perception through various states of awareness, the subtle dimensions of reality.

Perhaps the one music therapist who has most consistently created and developed a dialogue around issues of conciousness over the years is Helen Bonny. Her written works contain many guideposts for us to continue to follow.

The new physics supports our work as well. It redefines time and space, and in so doing moves toward music. It focuses on "process." Music therapists like Charles Eagle and his associates are developing a healthy dialogue in this community.

The world of psychology will remain an obvious place for dialogue. Even Ruud in his work *Music Therapy and its Relationship to Current Treatment Theories* describes our connections to psychological, communication and learning theories. We have gathered a portion of music therapy literature which views the music therapy experience through outside treatment models such as Boxill's *Music Therapy for the Developmentally Disabled* and Mary Priestly's *Music Therapy in Action*. The journals of music therapy have many articles which address important links to psychological and educational models.

Music therapists are quite naturally attracted to the worlds of personality theory, music education, human development and the list goes on and on.

There is a vast array of possibility for dialogue. There will be a huge encyclopedia of information available if we continue to pursue these connections to other fields. It is an exciting vista for our future development.

The fundamental statement of the *Field of Play* is that beauty exists everywhere. It is essentially in the nature of human form. We are limited in our perception of the vast beauty which does exist by the fragility of our human condition. We defend and hold back. We block. When we block, we often indiscriminately block our perception of beauty. Here we examine a way of opening the doors of perception of our therapeutic systems in order to allow the vision of this beauty to inform the manner in which we guide and facilitate human growth and development. In this sense, it is a powerful commitment to human potential.

Beauty exists equally in those who are disfigured and traumatized as it does in a therapist, or any other person whom the society may label as "healthy" or beautiful according to standards set by society-at-large. The *Field of Play* finds its source in the creative process and how this process might facilitate an expansion into even more beauty. It appreciates the power of a supportive field of loving and creating in sound.

The *Field of Play* suggests an attention to subtleties, quiet and implicit non-verbal cues, which communicate the natural healing patterns of the human person and imply an order which can guide and inform us into the best movement, which will lead us into wholeness.

Postcript

If language is to grow into a vehicle of thought, an expression of concepts and judgements, this evolution can be achieved only at the price of forgoing the wealth and fullness of immediate experience. In the end, what is left of the concrete sense and feeling content it once possessed is little more than a bare skeleton. But there is one intellectual realm in which the word not only preserves its original creative power, but is ever renewing it; in which it undergoes a sort of palingenesis, at once a sensuous and a spiritual reincarnation. This regeneration is achieved as language becomes an avenue of artistic expression. Here it recovers the fullness of life; but it is no longer a life mythically bound and fettered but an aesthetically liberated life.
(From Ernst Cassirer, *Language and Myth*)

The Blue Room

I took my place in the Blue Room, wearing a white gown with soft folds. In a time beyond the edge, I was born to dwell there.

The Blue Room is a temple of another time. Does it come to me in a dream or as a memory deep in the center of a Sacred Journey I left so long ago?

I am always waiting here with calm anticipation. The temple is full of silent sound. I guard the space. I walk this Beauty Way. I wait and breathe. The temple is a chamber of sound. An alchemist has poured a magical fluid into the stones of the walls. No instruments are necessary here—only prayer and breath and waiting which lives on the other side of time.

There are no gongs, no drums, no voices chanting long into the night. Yet I can breathe the sound of the cosmic soul. We all exist here.

Everything is blue and the air is pregnant. It is a container for loving and creating. Any healing sound which needs to be made lives here in these walls. Walking in the space, being in the space calls forth the great tone. To be is enough. To wait is enough. To love and create is all that exists here. It is immediate and present at all times.

Yet one would hear not a sound, would see not a thing. The air in the Blue Room is full of light and translucent in its hew.

Within this room can be heard the sound of the stars and planets as they make their journey through space. There are sounds of children laughing. The rustling of leaves in the wind. There is the sound of tears from the pool of grief. There is the sound of great anger as it rises out of the belly of the Earth herself. Even the sound of a rainbow is heard within these walls. The ancient drums and chants. The water.

Yet there is only soft breathing here. We breathe sound.

I hear birds outside the temple now. There are hundreds of birds of every kind and the Great Wind.

The Blue Room is a place beyond the Crystal Edge. It is a healing space in the landscape of my imaginings. Grandmother has told me that it is a dream and many other things as well.

"And must you always strive to understand?" she has said. "Can you not just believe the truth?"

In Blue Room we believe that **Music is taking care of Sound.**

Reading List

This reading list is a collection of works which have influenced the development of material in *The Field of Play*. The writers and thinkers represented here have inspired the ideas and concepts in both general and specific ways. Parts or pieces or wholes of their works are found as direct references and as indirect references. I am grateful to all of these authors for extending their ideas to me and I encourage you to explore them in your own way.

Achterberger, J. (1985) *Imagery in healing.* Boston and London: Shambhala.

Altshuler, I. (1948). A psychiatrist's experience with music as a therapeutic agent. In D. Schullian & M. Schoen (Eds.), *Music and medicine.* New York: Books for Libraries Press.

Alvin, J. (1982). Free improvisation in individual therapy. *British Journal of Music Therapy*, 13(2).

American Psychiatric Association. (1979). *The use of the creative arts in therapy.* Washington, D.C.

Argüelles, J. (1984). *Earth ascending: An illustrated treatise on the law governing whole systems.* Boulder and London: Shambhala.

Argüelles, J. (1975). *The transformative vision.* Boulder and London: Shambhala.

Arnold, E. (translation) *Bhagavad Gita: the song celestial.* New York: The Heritage Press.

Asmus, E.P., & Gilbert, J.P. (1981). A client-centered model of therapeutic intervention. *Journal of Music Therapy, XVIII.*

Assagioli, R. (1965). *Psychosynthesis.* New York: Penguin Books.

Barclay, M. (1987) A Contribution to a theory of Music Therapy: Additional Phenomenological Perspectives on Gestalt Qualitat and Transitional Phenomenon. *The Journal of Music Therapy*, Vol XXIV, No. 4.

Bateson, G. (1979) *Mind and Nature: a necessary unity.* New York: Bantam Books.

Baumel, L. (1973, Summer). Psychiatrist as music therapist. *Journal of Music Therapy, X.*

Bentov, I. (1977). *Stalking the wild pendulum.* New York: Bantam Books.

Berg, R.E., & Stork, D.G. (1982). *The physics of sound.* New Jersey: Prentice Hall.

Bly, R. (1980) *News of the universe.* San Fransisco: Sierra Club Books.

Bohm, D. (1980). *Wholeness and the implicate order.* Boston, MA: Routledge and Kegan Paul.

Bonny, H. (1984). *The musical lifeline: Present perspective and future possibilities.* Proceedings of the 11th Annual Conference of the Canadian Association for Music Therapy. Woodstock, Ontario.

Bonny, H. (1985, November 24). *Music: The language of immediacy.* Presentation for the National Conference of Art Therapies Assocation.

Bonny, H. (1978). *The role of taped music programs in the GIM process.* Baltimore, MD: ICM Books.

Bonny, H., & Savary, L. (1973). *Music and your mind.* New York: Harper and Row.

Bonny, H., & Walter N.P. (1972). The use of music in psychedelic (LSD) psychotherapy. *Journal of Music Therapy, IX.*

Boxill, E.H. (1985). *Music therapy for the developmentally disabled.* Rockville, MD: Aspen Systems Corporation.

Brain/Mind Bulletin, 1985, 10 (9,10,12).

Braswell, C. et al. (1979, Spring). A survey of clinical practice in music therapy. *Journal of Music Therapy, XVI(1).*

Burger, T. (1976). *Max Weber's theory of concept formation.* Durham, NC: Duke University Press.

Burrows, D. (1982). *The sound of thought.* 1982 New York Symposium paper.

Campbell, J. (1949) *Hero with a thousand faces.* Princeton: Princeton University Press.

Campbell, J. (1973). *Myths to live by.* New York: Bantam Books.

Capra, F. (1982) *The turning point.* New York: Bantom Books.

Cassirer, E. (1955) *The philosophy of symbolic forms.* Nw Haven and London: Yale University Press.

Cassirer, E. (1946) *Language and myth.* New York: Dover Publications Inc.

Casteneda, C. (1987) *The power of silence.* New York: Simon and Shuster.

Castaneda, C. *A Separate Reality.*

Chand, D. (1980) *The samaveda.* (trans.) New Delhi: Munshiram Manobarlal Publications Private Ltd.

Chetanananda, Swami. (1985). The symphony of life. *The American Theosophist.* Wheaton, IL: The Theosophist Press.

Churchill, G. (1986). *The binary triplet configuration in healing and wholeness.* Presented to The Institute for Religion and Wholeness, Claremont School of Theology, Claremont, CA.

Corsini, R. (1979). *Current psychotherapies.* Itasca, IL: F.E. Peacock Publishers, Inc.

Csikszentmihalyi, M. (1975). *Beyond boredom and anxiety.* San Francisco, CA: Jossey-Bass.

Csikszentmihalyi, M. (1978). Attention and the holistic approach to behavior. In K.S. Pape & S.L. Singer (Eds.), *The stream of consicousness.* New York: Plenum.

Dahlhaus, C. (1976). *Esthetics of music.* New York: Cambridge University Press.

d'Aquili, E., Laughlin, C., & McManus, J. (1979). *The spectrum of ritual.* New York: Columbia University Press.

De Bono, E. (1967). *New think.* New York: Abon Books.

De Chardin, P.T. (1962). *Human energy.* New York: Harcourt, Brace and Jovanovich.

De Chardin, P.T. (1959). *The phenomenon of man.* New York: Harper and Bros.

Deutsch, M., & Krauss, R.M. (1965). *Theories in social psychology.* New York: Basic Books.

Dossey, L. (1982). *Space, time and medicine.* Boulder, CO: Shambhala.

Douglass, B., & Moustakas, C. (1985, Summer). Heuristic inquiry: The internal search to know. *Journal of Humanistic Psychology, 25*(3).

Drury, N. (1985). *Music for inner space.* San Leandro, CA: Prism Press.

Dubois, R. (1974). *Beast of angel?* New York: Charles Scribner's Sons.

Dufrenne, M. (1973). *The phenomenology of aesthetic experience.* Evanston, IL: Northwestern University Press.

Eagle, C. (1972). Music and LSD: An empirical study. *Journal of Music Therapy, IX*(1).

Eagle, C. (Ed.). (1978, 1976). *The music therapy index* (Vols 1 and 2). Lawrence, KS: National Association for Music Therapy.

Eagle, C. (1982). *Some implications of new physics for music therapy.* New York: Symposium.

Eckblad, G. (1981). *Sceme theory: A conceptual framework for cognitive-motivational processes.* London and New York: Academic Press.

Eiseley, L. (1961). *The man who saw through time.* New York: Charles Scribner's Sons.

Eisner, E. (1981, April). One the differences between scientific and artistic approaches to qualitative research. *Educational Researcher.*

Eliade, M. (1963). *Myth and reality.* New York: Harper and Row.

Ellerbroek, W.C. (1978, Spring). Language, thought and disease. *Co-Evolution Quarterly, 17.*

Feder, E., & Feder, B. (1981). *The expressive arts therapies.* Englewood Cliffs, NJ: Prentice-Hall.

Feld, S. (1982) *Sound and sentiment.* Philadelphia: University of Pennsylvania Press.

Fogerty, E. (1936). *Rhythm*. London: George Allen and Unwin Ltd.

Franz, K. (1978). *Music in the human ecosystem*. Presentation for the Canadian Association for Music Therapy, Vancouver, B.C.

Funk, J. (1983) Music and fourfold vision. *Revision*. Spring.

Gasset, Ortega Y. (1956). *The dehumanization of art*. Garden City, NJ: Doubleday.

Gaston, E.T. (1968). *Music in therapy*. New York: The Macmillan Co., 1968.

Gaston, E.T., & Eagle, C.T. (1970, Spring). The function of music in LSD therapy for alcoholic patients. *Journal of Music Therapy, VII*(1).

Gfeller, K.E. (1984). Prominent theories in learning disabilities and implications for music therapy methodology. *Music Therapy Perspectives*, 2(1).

Godwin, J. (1985). Hearing secret harmonies. *The American Theosophist*. Wheaton, IL: The Theosophist Press.

Gray, W., & Laviolette, P. (1983). *Man-environment-systems, 9*(1).

Greenberg, J.R., & Mitchell, S.A. (1983). *Object relations in psycho analytic theory*. Cambridge, MA: Harvard University Press.

Grimes, R.L. (1982). *Beginning in ritual studies*. Washington, D.C.:University Press of America.

Grinder, J., & Bandler, R. (1981). *Trance-formations*. Moab, UT: Real People Press.

Grof, S. (1985) *Beyond the Brain*. New York: State University of New York Press.

Grof, S. *Dimensions of consciousness: New cartography of the human psyche*. Unpublished paper.

Grossmann, R. (1984). *Phenomenology and existentialism: An introduction*. London: Routledge and Kegan Paul.

Hall, M. (1955). *The therapeutic use of music*. Los Angeles, CA: The philosophical Research Society, Inc.

Hampden-Turner, C. (1981). *Maps of the mind*. New York: Collier Books.

Hanna, J.L. (1980). *To dance is human*. Austin, TX: University of Texas Press.

Harman, W., & Rheingold, H. (1984). *Higher creativity*. Los Angeles, CA: Jeremy P. Tarcher, Inc.

Heidegger, M. (1971) *Poetry, Language, Thought*. New York: Harper Colophon Books.

Hegel, G.W.F. (1977). *Phenomenology of spirit*. New York: Harper Colophon Books.

Highwater, J. (1981). *The primal mind*. New York: Harper and Row.

Hodges, D. (1980). *Handbook of music psychology*. Lawrence, KS: NAMT.

Husserl, E. (1965). *Phenomenology and the crisis of philosophy.* New York: Harper and Row.

Huxley, A. (1973). Integrated education. *Synthesis,* 3-4.

Huxley, A. (1954). *The doors of perception.* New York: Harper and Row.

Idhe, D. (1986) *Consequences of phenomenology.* New York: State University of New York Press.

Idhe, D. (1973) *Sense and significance.* Atlantic Highlands, New Jersey: Humanities Press.

Iyer, R. (1984) *Noetic psychology.* London: Concord Grove Press.

Jablanszy, L. (1980). *The effect of sound of organisms-neural response to musical stimuli.* Proceedings of the Seventh Annual Conference of the Canadian Association for Music Therapy, 2, Woodstock, Ontario.

James, M. (1984). Sensory integration. A theory for therapy and research. *Journal of Music Therapy, XXI*(2).

Jantsch, E. (1981). *The self-organizing universe.* New York: Pergamon Press.

Jaynes, J. (1976). *The origin of consciousness in the breakdown of the bicameral mind.* Boston, MA Houghton Mifflin Co.

Jellison, J. (1976). Accuracy of temporal order recall for berbal and song digit-spans presented to right and left ears. *Journal of Music Therapy, XVII*(3).

Jilek, W. (1982) *Indian healing.* Surrey, B.C. Canada: Hancock House Publishers, Ltd.

Johnston, W. (1976) *Silent music.* San Fransisco: Harper and Row Publishers.

Jung, C.C. (1956). *Symbols of transformation.* Princeton, NJ: Princeton University Press.

Jung, C.G. (1965) *Memories, dreams and reflections.* New York: Vintage Books.

Kaleidoscope: Perspectives on music therapy. (1983). Toronto: Ontario Institute for Studies in Education.

Kalff, D. (1980). *Sandplay.* Santa Monica, CA: Sigo Press.

Kapferer, B. (Ed.). (1979). *Social analysis: The power of ritual (#1).* Adelaide, South Australia: University of Adelaide.

Kaplan,L. (1978) *Oneness and Separateness: From Infant to Individual.* New York: Simon and Shuster.

Katz, R. (1982). *Boiling energy.* Boston: Harvard University Press.

Kenny, C. (1987) *The Field of Play: A theoretical study of music therapy process.* Dissertation, The Fielding Institute.

Kenny, C. (1985). Music: a whole systems approach. *Music Therapy, 5(1),* 3-11.

Kenny, C. (1983). *Phenomenological research: A promise for the healing arts.* Proceedings of the 10th Annual Conference of the Canadian

150   *Reading List*

Association for Music Therapy, Toronto.

Kenny, C. (1982A). *The essence of music and therapy.* Paper for the International Symposium on Music in the Life of Man: Toward a Theory of Music Therapy, New York.

Kenny, C. (1982B). *The Mythic Artery: The Magic of Music Therapy.* Atascadero, Ca: Ridgeview Publishing Co.

Khan, H.I. (1983). *The music of life.* Sante Fe, NM: Omega Press.

Knobloch, F. et. al. (1964) Musical experience as interpersonal process. *Psychiatry: Journal for the study of interpersonal processes.* vol. 27.

Kockelmans, J. (1967). *Phenomenology.* New York: Doubleday and Co., Inc.

Kohut, H., & Levavie, S. (1969). On the enjoyment of listening to music. *Psychoanalytic Quarterly, 23(1).*

Knobloch, F. (1964). Musical experience as interpersonal process. *Journal for the Study of Interpersonal Processes, 27.*

Koestenbaum, P. (1978). *The new image of the person: The theory and practice of clinical philosophy.* Westport, Ct: Greenwood press, Inc.

Koestler, A. (1978). *Janus.* New York: Vintage Books.

Kuhn, T. (1962). *The structure of scientific revolutions.* Chicago, IL: University of Chicago Press.

Kupfer, J.H. (1983). *Art as experience.* Albany, NY: State University of New York.

Langer, S. (1972). *Mind: An essay on human feeling.* Baltimore, MD: Johns Hopkins University Press.

Larsen, S. (1976). *The shaman's doorway.* New York: Harper and Row.

Langer, S. (1942). *Philosophy in a new key.* Cambridge, MA: Harvard University Press.

Laszlo, E. (1972A). *The relevance of general systems theory.* New York: George Braziller.

Laszlo, E. (1972B). *The systems view of the world.* New York: George Braziller.

LeBlanc, A. (1982). An interactive theory of music preference. *Journal of Music Therapy, XIX(1).*

Leonard, G. (1978). *The silent pulse.* New York: E.P. Dutton.

Lerner, R. (1976) *Concepts and theories of human development.* Menlo Park, CA: Addison-Wesley Publishing Co.

LeShan, L. and Margenau, H. (1982) *Einstein's space and Van Gogh's sky.* New York: MacMillan Publishing Co., Inc.

LeShan, L. (1966) *The medium, the mystic and the physicist.* New York: ne Books.

Levey, J. (1987) *The Fine arts of relaxation, concentration and meditation.* London: Wisdom Publications.

Lewin, K. (1935). *Dynamic theory of personality.* New York: McGraw-Hill.

Livesey, L. (1972). Noetic planning: The need to know, but what? *The relevance of general systems theory.* New York: George Braziller.

Madison, Gary Brent. *The Phenomenology of Merleau-Ponty.*

Madson, C. (1975). A comparison of music as reinforcement for correct mathematical responses versus music as reinforcement for attentiveness. *Journal of Music Therapy, XII(2).*

Madson, C. (1978). Research on research: An evaluation of research presentations. *Journal of Music Therapy, XV(2).*

Malson, L. (1980-81). Music, meaning and madness: A conversation with Jean-Paul Sartre. *Review of Existential Psychology and Psychiatry,* XVII(1).

Marcuse, H. (1962). *Eros and civilization.* New York: Vintage Books.

Maslow, A. (1962). *The farther reaches of human nature.* New York: The Viking Press.

Maslow, A. *Toward a psychology of being.* Princeton, NJ: D. Van Nostrand Co., Inc.

May, R. (1985). *My quest for beauty.* New York: Saybrook publishing Co.

McLaughlin, T. (1970). *Music and communication.* London: Faber and Faber.

McMaster, N. (1976, Winter). A description of improvisation for children with behavioral problems at the Burnaby Mental Health Center Preschool Plus. *The Journal of the Canadian Association for Music Therapy, 4(1).*

McWhinney, W. (1989). *Of Paradigms and Systems Theories.* Fielding Institute.

McWhinney, W. (1984, Fall). Alternative realities. *Journal of Humanistic Psychology, 24(4).*

Merleau-Ponty. (1973A). *Adventures of the dialectic.* Evanston, IL: Northwestern University Press.

Merleau-Ponty, M. (1973B) *Consciousness and the acquisition of language.* Evenston: Northwestern University Press.

Merleau-Ponty, M. (1973C) *The prose of the world.* Evanston: Northwestern University Press.

Michel, D. (1976). *Music therapy.* Springfield, IL: Charles C. Thomas.

Michel, D.E. (1971). Music therapy: An idea whose time has arrived around the world. *Journal of Music Therapy, VIII(3).*

Miller, J. (1983). *States of mind.* New York: Pantheon Books.

Mishlove, J. (1975). *The roots of consciousness.* New York: Random House.

Munro, S. (1984). *Music therapy in palliative care.* St. Louis, MO: Magna-Music Baton.

Muses, C. (1972). A new way of altering consciousness: Manual of dynamic resonance meditation. *The Journal for the Study of Consciousness, 5(2).*

Nicholas, M., & Gilbert, J.P. (1980). Research in music therapy: A survey of music therapists's attitudes and knowledge. *Journal of Music Therapy, XVII(4)*.

Nordoff, P., & Robbins, C. (1977). *Creative music therapy*. New York: The John Day Co.

Nordoff, P., & Robbins, C. (1971). *Therapy in music for handicapped children*. London: Victor Gollanez Ltd.

Nowicki, A., & Trevisan, L.A. (1978). *Beyond the sound.* Santa Barbara, CA: Nowicki/Trevisan.

Noy, P. (1967). The psychodynamic meaning of music. *Journal of Music Therapy, IV(3)*.

Nuttin, J. (1984). *Motivation, planning and action: A relational theory of behavior dynamics*. Hillsdale, NY: Leuren University Press:, Larence Erlbaum Association.

Orff, G. 91974). *The Orff music therapy*. New York: Schott Music Corp.

Ornstein, R. (1972). *The psychology of consciousness*. New York: Penguin Books.

Packer, M.J. (1985, October). Hermeneutic inquiry in the study of human conduct. *American Psychologist.*

Polanyi, M. (1946) *Science, faith and society*. Chicago and London: The University of Chicago Press.

Polanyi, M. (1958). *Personal knowledge*. New York: Harper and Row.

Priestly, M. (1978). Counter-transference in analytical music therapy. *British Journal of Music Therapy, 9(3)*.

Priestly, M. (1975). *Music therapy in action*. London: Constable.

Prigogine, I. (1984) *Order out of chaos*. New York: Bantam Books.

Proceedings from the International Study Group on a Theory of Music Therapy, Dallas, 1980.

Proceedings from the International Symposium on Music in the Life of Man: Toward a Theory of Music Therapy, New York University, 1982.

Proceedings of the World Congress of Music Therapy, Paris: l'Association Francaise de Musico-therapie, 1983.

Raines, K. (1983). Recovering a Common Language. *Parabola*, Vol III, 3 (August, 1983).

Raphael. (1982). *The starseed transmissions: An extraterrestrial report.* UniSun.

Rapoport, A. (1967). *Operational philosophy*. New York: John Wiley and Sons.

Rider, M., & Eagle, C. (in publication). Rhythmic entrainment as a mechanism for learning in music therapy. In J. Evens & M. Clynes, *Rhythm in language, learning and other life experience*.

Robbins, A. (1980). *Expressive therapy: A creative arts approach to depth-oriented treatment.* New York: Human Sciences press.

Robbins, T. (1984). *Jitterbug perfume.* New York: Bantam Books.

Robbins, A. (1987) *The artist as therapist.* New York: Human Sciences Press, Inc.

Rogers, C. (1961). *On becoming a person.* Boston: Houghton Mifflin Co.

Rudhyar, D. (1979). *Beyond individualism.* Wheaton, IL: The Theosophical Publishing House.

Rudhyar, D. (1982). *The magic of tone and the art of music.* Boulder and London: Shambhala.

Ruud, E. (1980). *Music therapy and its relationship to current treatment theories.* St. Louis, MO: Magna-Music Baton.

Ruud, E. (1986) *Music and health.* Copenhagen: Norsk Musikforlag.

Samples, B. (1976). *The metaphoric mind.* Reading, MA: Addison-Wesley Publishing Co.

Sandner, D. (1979). *Navaho symbols of healing.* New York: Harcourt, Brace and Jovanovich.

Sanford, J. *Healing and wholeness.* New York: Paulist Press.

Santayana, G. (1955). *The sense of beauty.* New York: Dover Publications, Inc.

Satre, J.P. (1963). *Search for a method.* New York: Knopf.

Shafranske, E., & Gorsuch, R. (1984). Factors associated with the perception of spirituality in psychotherapy. *Journal of Transpersonal Psychology, 16(2).*

Shaughnessy, J. (1973). *The roots of ritual.* Grand Rapids, MI: William B. Erdmans Publishing Co.

Sheldrake, R. (1981). *A new science of life.* Los Angeles, CA: J.P. Tarcher, Inc.

Solomon, A., & Heller, G. (1982). Historical research in music therapy: An important avenue for study in the profession. *Journal of Music Therapy, XIX(3).*

Spiegelberg, H. (1972). *Phenomenology in psychology and psychiatry.* Evanston, IL: Northwestern University Press.

Stephens, G. (1983). The use of improvisation for developing relatedness in the adult client. *Music Therapy, 3(1).*

Stein, M. (Ed.). (1982). *Jungian analysis.* LaSalle and London: Open Court.

Strong, M. (1948) *The Letters of the Scattered Brotherhood.* Harper and Rowe.

Sudnow, D. (1978) *Ways of the hands.* New York: Harper Colophon Books.

Sullivan, D. (1927). *Beethoven-His Spiritual Development.* Vintage Books.

Suzuki, S. (1969). *Nutured by love.* New York: Exposition Press.

Szent-Gyoergyi, A. (1974, Spring). Drive in living matter to perfect itself. *Synthesis.*

Tarthang, T. (1977). *Time, space and knowledge.* Emeryville, CA: Dharma

Publishing.

Task panel reports. (1978). President's Commission on Mental Health (Vol. IV). Washington, D.C.

Tesch, R. (1980). *Phenomenological research: Naturalistic inquiry.* Santa Barbara, CA: The Fielding Institute.

Thaut, M. (1984). A music therapy treatment model for autistic children. *Music Therapy Perspectives.* 1(4).

Tolstoy, L. (1960). *What is art?* Indianapolis, IN: Bobbs-Merrill Educational Publishing Co.

Troup, M. (1979, Summer). The scope of music therapy: Toward a method of assessment. British Journal of Music Therapy, 10(2).

Trungpa, C. (1984) *Shambhala: The Sacred Path of the Warrior.* New York: Bantam Books.

Turner, V. (1969). *The ritual process: Structure and anti-structure.* New York: Cornell University Press.

Tyson, F. (1981). *Psychiatric music therapy.* New York: Fred Widner and Sons Printers, Inc.

Vash, C. (1981). *The psychology of the disabled.* New York: Springer Publishing Co.

Vargiu, J. (1972). Creativity. *Synthesis, 3-4.*

Von Franz, M.L. (1978). *Time: Rhythm and repose.* New York: Hudson and Thames.

Walsh, R. (1983, Spring). The conciousness disciplines. *Journal of Humanistic Psychology, 23(2).*

Ware, Bishop K. (1985). Image and likeness. *Parabola: Wholeness, X(1).*

Watkins, M. (1984) *Waking Dreams.* Dallas: Spring Publications, Inc.

Weber, R. (1982). Field conciousness and field ethics. *The holographic paradigm and other paradoxes.* Boulder and London: Shambhala Publications, Inc.

Wetzler, L.A. (1977). *A phenomenological investigation of becoming and being relaxed through listening to music.* Dissertation proposal, Department of Psychology, Duquesne University.

Wheeler, B. (1982). *Aspects of the musical experience and man.* Paper for the International Synposiun on Music in the Life of Man: Toward a Theory of Music Therapy, New York.

Whitehead, A. (1938) *Modes of thought.* New York: The Free Press.

Whone, H. (1980). Sound and music as the root of our existence. *Parabola: Music, Sound, Silence, V(2).*

Wilber, K. (1984A, Spring). Of shadows and symbols: Physics and mysticism. *Revision, 7(1).*

Wilber, K. (1984B, Spring). Sheldrake's theory of morphogensis. *Journal of Humanistic Psychology, 24(2).*

Wilber, K. (1983). *Eye to eye.* New York: Anchor Press, Doubleday.

Wilber, K. (1982). *The holographic paradigm and other paradoxes.*

Shambala.

Wilber, K. (1980). *The Atman project.* Wheaton, IL: The Theosophical Publishing House.

Winnecott, D.W. (1971). *Playing and reality.* New York: Basic books.

Winnecott, D.W. (1975). *Through paediatrics to psycho-analysis.* New York: Basic books.

Witherspoon, G. (1977). *Language and art in the Navaho universe.*

Wolpow, R. (1976). The independent effects of contingent social and academic approval upon the musical on-task and performance behaviors of profoundly retarded adults. *Journal of Music Therapy, XIII(1).*

Yalom, I. (1980). *Existential psychology.* New York: Basic Books.

Young, A. (1984, Spring). Are the foundations of science adequate? *Revision, 7(1).*

Young, A. (1976). *The geometry of meaning.* San Fransisco, CA: Robert Briggs Association.

Young, A. (1976). *The reflexive universe.* San Fransisco, CA: Robert Briggs Publishing.